THE FARMER'S SLAUGHTER (BOOK 1)

A HARLEY AND DAVIDSON MYSTERY

LILIANA HART

LOUIS SCOTT

Jai Clark -
Thank you dearly for the friendship we've grown. We appreciate your investment of time and creativity in our lives, and thanks to you, the small town of Rusty Gun, Texas officially becomes somewhere that someone calls home.
Your friends,
Scott & Liliana

To our kids -
Stop calling us. Yes, we are home, but we're trying to get a little adult time in between driving y'all to all of your activities. And by adult time, we mean napping. We love you anyway.

CHAPTER ONE

"They call him Hammerin' Hank," Heather said, waggling her eyebrows. "I wonder what it is he hammers?"

Agatha buried her face in the plastic menu, not particularly interested in the man Heather had targeted to be her next ex-husband. Especially since the man in question was new in Agatha's neighborhood. Not that she'd spent a lot of time peeping through her blinds and down the corner at him. It was just neighborly curiosity. But the man definitely had a story.

The cracked vinyl seat of the booth scratched her legs, and she regretted the skirt she'd put on that morning, but it had been one of the only clean things left in her closet. So it was either the skirt or the cocktail dress she'd worn at a New Year's party several years before. The skirt wasn't so bad. It was made out of soft cotton, plus it had pockets, which was the best invention in the history of the runway, in her opinion.

The problem with wearing a skirt was you had to do it justice. Skirts required a certain cute factor that took a little bit of effort. So she'd put on a black and white striped stretchy top and pulled her dark hair into a loose ponytail with a few free-flying wisps like Heather had showed her. And then she'd added dangly black earrings because she figured she might as well go all out. The only thing she was missing was her black Toms, which were buried in the mud along with her pride, so she'd opted for a pair of black ballet flats instead.

The problem with effort was that Agatha had no time for it. In fact, she had no time for lunch with Heather either, but guilt had her meeting her friend even though deadline was calling. She'd been running a scene through her head for the last two days, and it still wasn't right.

"Maybe he's a contractor," she said, feeling guilty for ignoring her friend. "Or maybe he works on the railroad. Or *maybe* he's a vampire hunter and hammers stakes into their hearts."

Heather swatted away Agatha's menu, so she had no choice but to engage face to face. "You're no fun, Agatha. Come on, tell me what you think about him. You can't tell me you haven't noticed him. You're about the nosiest person I've ever met."

"I'm doing character research," Agatha said dryly.

"Sure you are. Please," she begged. "You can always size people up way better than I can."

"A frozen slab of beef can size people up better than you can. I've never seen anyone who has such bad taste in men."

Which was another reason Agatha wasn't particularly interested in her new neighbor. If Heather picked him, he was bad news.

"Hush up, Agatha," Heather said. "There was nothing wrong with Troy. He was a nice man."

"And then you made him crazy and he drove his car

through that liquor store. Maybe you need to join a nunnery and leave the male population in peace. They have enough trouble as it is without throwing you in the mix."

Heather laughed, a long scarlet nail tapping on the side of her Diet Coke. "Sugar, what fun would that be? God put women on earth to drive men crazy. I'm just doing my duty."

Agatha was pretty sure God hadn't expected Heather to go through husbands like Dixie cups, but there was no use telling her friend that. She was bound and determined to find husband number five before the year was out.

In her opinion, Heather Cartwright should come with a big warning label strapped around her neck. A place like Rusty Gun, Texas wasn't a big enough hunting ground for a woman like Heather, which was why she'd extended her web clear into Austin.

Since Heather had received a rather nice settlement from husband number one, she hadn't had to worry about things like a normal nine to five job. Mostly, she spent her days going to the spa and the gym. According to Heather, maintenance was key for husband hunting. And it took effort to maintain a body you could bounce quarters off, a year-round tan, white blonde hair, and breasts that acted as their own flotation devices.

"All I'm saying is the man has barely moved to town," Agatha said. "He's still got boxes stacked sky-high in his garage. Give him a chance to settle in before you seduce him."

"I do like a mature man," Heather said, leaning back in the booth so she was displayed to her best advantage. "They know things, if you get my drift."

She was staring at the man like he was an all-day sucker, and Agatha had to hand it to the guy, he was doing a darned good job at ignoring them. Most men were sitting up ready to beg by the time Heather gave them that look.

"Are you ready to order?" Agatha asked. "I need to eat and run. I've got too much work to do to play today."

"You do nothing but work. Taking a break every once in a while won't kill you."

"That's not how my brain works. When I'm in the middle of a book all I can think about is that book. It doesn't matter how hard I try to take a break. It doesn't work."

Heather stared at her like she'd grown two heads. Work was like a foreign language to Heather. And trying to explain the creative process was like trying to teach a chimpanzee rocket science.

"Penny," Agatha called out to the waitress. "We'd like to order now."

A girl not long out of high school seemed surprised to hear her name called. Agatha immediately felt empathy for the girl. She was one of those who was aged beyond her years, but whatever curveballs life had continued to throw at her, she was still standing.

The girl flushed red and made her way to the table, her pad in hand. "I didn't realize you knew my name," she said, wide-eyed as she stared at Agatha. "I've read all your books. Even the newest one. I'm such a huge fan. Maybe you could sign my apron?"

"Oh," Agatha said, shifting in her seat uncomfortably. "Thank you, that's very sweet. I've got an extra copy of the book in my bag if you'd like me to sign that for you."

"Oh, wow, Ms. Harley, that would be fantastic. Wait until I tell my boyfriend. He's a big fan too."

"I'll have the chicken Caesar salad," Heather said, rolling her eyes at Agatha. "I've got this dress I have to fit into tonight, and you know how carbs make me bloated."

Agatha half-listened to Heather as she dug around in her bag for the book and then signed it, passing it over to Penny.

"You're the best," Penny gushed. "Everyone in town always talks about how nice you are, even though you keep to yourself all the time. There's been a time or two a reporter or fan has shown up here looking to find where you live, but we know how to protect our own in Rusty Gun."

All Agatha could do was nod, and then she finally said, "I'll have the same as Heather's having."

Agatha hated salads, but she couldn't think beyond the panic that had taken hold of her at Penny's words. The whole town knew who she was. Who she *really* was. Of course everyone knew she was Agatha Harley. She'd grown up in Rusty Gun. But there was a reason she wrote under the name A.C. Riddle and had a security system Fort Knox would be proud of. She'd gone above and beyond to make sure her identity was kept secret. She didn't do book signings. There were no pictures on her website or the dust jackets of her books. She lived in anonymity, and she liked it that way.

Sure, there were a handful of people who knew her author name. She didn't keep her profession a secret. But most people didn't care enough to delve too deep. The only times she had to give her pen name was when she needed to prove her credibility to get into some places to further her research. This new information was definitely something to think about.

She and Heather sat in the corner booth by the front window, and Agatha traced a finger over the backwards, hand-painted lettering on the glass, advertising the world's best barbecue and fried green tomatoes. The café was on the corner of Main Street, so she had a great view of the chaos taking place out in the parking lot. Whoever had mapped out the city of Rusty Gun had done a terrible job, but a hundred and fifty years later, it was still entertaining to watch.

Rusty Gun was just like Tombstone, Arizona, only there hadn't been any famous lawmen or outlaws to make a name for the town after the infamous shootout of 1886. In fact, both the lawmen and the outlaws had been terrible shots, and everyone had walked away with no more than a scratch on them, but it was all about the media spin. Unfortunately, Rusty Gun hadn't spun it right, and it had come close to not existing at all after the railroads were built and bypassed the town. Rusty Gun even had its own version of the O.K. Corral, but somehow the B.O. Corral—short for Boggs and Oliver—didn't have the same ring to it.

The street was cobbled and the old hitching posts were still intact. It looked like a wild west saloon town, which was one of the reasons she loved it so much. Every person and every place had a story, and telling stories was her business.

But for a one-horse town—or a one-stoplight town in the case of Rusty Gun—the traffic was ridiculous. The parking was haphazard at best, the lines crooked and different widths, and no one was ever really sure which direction to go on the traffic circle that surrounded the statue of John Wayne. Legend had it he'd passed through town once or twice on his way to Austin, and for a town of 1800 people that didn't have a claim to fame, a statue of the Duke was more than sufficient.

"Darn, that man is stubborn," Heather said pouting. "He hasn't even looked at me once. I enjoy a little challenge from time to time, but there's no excuse for bad manners. He must be a Yankee."

"Umm...Heather?" Agatha said. "Did you park in front of the fire hydrant?"

"There was no place else to park," she said, waving away the concern. "It's not like we're going to be here much longer anyway. That fire hydrant is taking up a perfectly good parking space. There's absolutely no reason for them to put it right there."

"Except for the fact that there could be a fire and the whole of Main Street might burn down without it."

"If you ask me, this place is due for a little renovation anyway. It's like how when the forest burns down, it clears the land for new and better growth."

"How very progressive of you," Agatha said.

"Duncan was a city manager. He taught me a lot before his untimely death."

Duncan was Heather's third husband. He'd embezzled a couple of million dollars over the ten years he'd worked for the city of Austin, and he'd driven his Porsche right over the edge of a cliff and into the Brazos river, though the final report had said he'd lost control of the car instead of intentionally taken his life, so Heather had made out good with the life insurance policy.

Heather turned her attention back to Hammerin' Hank. "Come on, Agatha. Size him up for me. He looks a little rough around the edges, but I need something a little different. All those slick and polished men get old after a while. It's nothing but champagne and tuxes. I want a blue-collar man. Someone that knows how to get his hands dirty."

"Yeah, that sounds just like your type," Agatha said rolling her eyes.

"Please?" Heather asked, batting her baby-blues. Not that it worked on Agatha. She'd been doing the same thing since they were in kindergarten. But Agatha sighed and turned toward her new neighbor.

And instantly realized her mistake.

Lord, could she size him up all right. That was the problem. She didn't say she hadn't looked at the man. Only that she was uninterested. He definitely wasn't hard on the eyes. But she recognized a battered soul and a whole lot of baggage when she saw it. Seeing through the façade of people was part of her job.

"Fine," Agatha finally agreed. She scooted closer toward the window and angled her body so she had a better view of him, without making it seem like she was outright staring at him. "He's got a nice profile. Good genes and even features. Athletic build. He's definitely all man. I can appreciate a pair of shoulders like that."

"Go on," Heather urged. "Get to the good stuff."

"I'd say he's divorced," she said. "Not many men around here wear cargo shorts and Hawaiian shirts that have to go out in public with their wives. He's wearing the clothes, but he's not comfortable in them. Like they're a disguise. Or he's doing it on a dare."

"I can buy the man new clothes," Heather said. "Maybe you're right. Maybe they call him Hammerin' Hank because he's a construction worker. The thought of that man in a tool belt really gets my motor running."

"I don't know," Agatha said. "That doesn't feel right now that I'm getting a good look at him. He's definitely blue-collar. He's older. Maybe late forties. If he didn't have the silver at his temples I'd put him a decade younger."

Agatha narrowed her eyes and stared, like she could somehow see deeper if she only looked harder. And then he turned his head and their eyes met. Coal black eyes that looked like they'd stared down the devil and won. She was caught in the trap, and she gasped slightly, shaking her head to try and break the hold he had on her. And then he turned his attention back to his crossword puzzle and coffee and the spell was broken.

"Nope," Agatha said, shaking her head.

"What do you mean nope?" Heather asked.

"I mean don't waste your time. He's a cop."

"Oh, I've dated lots of cops," Heather said, waving away the concern.

"Not like this one you haven't. He'd chew you up and spit you out in a heartbeat. And if you think batting your eyelashes at a man like that is going to work you'd better come up with a new strategy."

Heather pouted, stirring her straw in her drink. "Well, maybe I can just sleep with him."

"I don't know, but it might not be a bad idea to up your life insurance policy. Am I still your beneficiary?"

"Ahem." Someone coughed next to them, and Agatha jumped, realizing they weren't alone.

Heat flushed her cheeks and she looked up into the amused eyes of Karl Johnson. She'd babysat him a couple of times before she graduated from high school. Rusty Gun was such a small town it was impossible not to know everyone. Kindergarten through twelfth grade was still all housed in the same building.

Karl wasn't a big man, only a couple of inches shorter than Agatha's five-foot-ten, but his posture made him seem much taller. He was stocky and muscular, a far cry from the skinny boy she once babysat, and his dark hair was shorn close to his skull. A thin mustache that seemed like a regrettable decision grew above his upper lip, and his tan uniform was pressed within an inch of its life, his duty belt snug around his hips. A tattoo in black ink showed just below his sleeve, but it was almost impossible to see unless you were staring since it was so close to the color of his skin.

"I don't mean to interrupt the latest episode of *The Bachelor*, but there's a pretty red Mercedez parked right in front of the fire hydrant out there."

He pulled out his ticket book and gave a pointed look to Heather.

"Come on, Karl," she said. "Don't be ridiculous. We're going to be in and out. You know that thing is a public nuisance."

"Now, Heather," he said, his wide smile showing a set of dimples. "You know there's only one public nuisance around here, and it isn't that little bitty fire hydrant."

Agatha snorted out a laugh and covered her mouth when Heather glared at her.

"Please, Karl," Heather begged. "You know I can't get another ticket. There's too many dadgum rules in this town. I'm tired of the police department making all its money off me. Can't I just write you a check that counts as a charitable contribution instead of it always going on my record?"

"I don't know about you, Agatha, but that sounds like bribing a police officer to me."

Agatha nodded. "Don't worry, Heather. I'll bail you out of jail."

"Shut up, Agatha."

"You better be glad Tyler Gunn's not on duty. He doesn't give anyone a break." Karl warned.

Penny came up at that moment with their food and set their salads in front of them.

"Man, I hate salads," Agatha said once Penny had left.

"Why'd you order it?" Karl asked.

"Long story."

"I'll tell you what, Heather," Karl said, putting up his

ticket book. "There's a spot that just opened up. Go move the car and we'll save taking away your license for another day."

Heather looked like she wanted to argue, but instead she glared at Karl and grabbed her Louis Vuitton handbag and her keys, scooting out of the booth with all the quiet rage of Scarlet O'Hara displeased with her servants.

"That woman scares the dickens out of me," Karl said, taking her seat once she'd left. "Can't seem to help myself though. It's fun messing with her."

Agatha shook her head and laughed. "You're playing with fire. Much like that mustache you're trying to grow."

"You like it?" he asked. "I think the mustache deserves a second chance at being in style."

"Unless you're Magnum P.I., that mustache is never going to be in style."

Penny came back with a cup of coffee for Karl. Agatha guessed he frequented the café so much that she knew what to bring him, because he hadn't ordered.

"So what's your interest in Hank Davidson?" he asked.

"He moved in down the street from me," Agatha said, fighting to steal another look at him. "Heather decided she was going to make him husband number five and asked me to size him up."

"I heard," he said, mouth twitching. "You did a good job. Sheriff Coil said he's a big city murder cop. He's been specially trained by the FBI to profile people."

"Oh, really?" she asked, her interest going up a notch. "What's a big city murder cop doing in Rusty Gun, Texas? There's definitely a story there."

"Not much of one," Karl said, shrugging. "I guess there comes a time when the evil the killers leave behind starts to stick to your soul and it's too hard to wash it off every day.

Sheriff said he retired and is just looking for a place to fade into existence. I guess when you're high-profile the bad guys eventually come looking for you."

The bell over the door rang again as Heather came back in, and Karl moved out of the seat to get out of her way, taking his coffee cup with him.

"You ladies have a good day," he said, winking at Heather and making her scowl. "Try to stay out of trouble."

CHAPTER TWO

SHE WASN'T STALKING. Really, she wasn't. It just so happened that it was impossible not to pass Hank's house on the way back to her own. And she wouldn't have stopped and stared at all if he hadn't looked like a fish out of water, or in his case, a cop out of *Krispy Kreme's*.

"I hope he didn't work undercover," Agatha murmured, bending down to stretch a couple of houses down. She was soaked with sweat and she was pretty sure her spandex was steaming her body. It would probably fall right off her body like a soup chicken when she undressed.

The temperature was brutal for an early morning, and she was thinking if this summer was already this brutal that she might find a cooler destination for the next couple of months.

She'd admired Hank's front landscaping for years. The Cooper's had owned the house before Hank had bought it, and they'd spent a lot of time making their simple, single-story cottage look like it belonged between the pages of a fairy tale.

Hank didn't look like he belonged in a fairy tale. He

looked like he belonged in an episode of The Sopranos. He stood in the front yard, legs slightly spread and the water hose in front of him like he was holding a pistol at the firing range. He was wearing a pair of black athletic shorts, a different patterned Hawaiian shirt, a pair of black socks, Birkenstocks, and a cannon strapped to his side.

He looked like a man who needed help. He was about the worst retired person she'd ever seen. And as luck would happen, she was a writer in need of help. She'd been in a slump for the last week, putting no more than a couple of paragraphs on the page, and she'd ended up erasing those. What she needed was inspiration. Sometimes all she needed to give her that extra push was to listen to other's experiences.

Ever since Karl had told her Hank had moved to Rusty Gun to retire more than a week ago, her mind hadn't stopped asking the question *Why?* A man like Hank Davidson, who was used to the constant adrenaline rush and life of the city, didn't just move to Nowhere, Texas without a pretty darn good reason.

She got moving again, determined to put her plan into motion. Yes, she would be using him shamelessly, but desperate times called for desperate measures.

"Just introduce yourself," she said. "You're friendly. And cops love you. Maybe it's because you think like they do, or maybe it's because you ply them with cookies. It doesn't matter. You've got charm."

She'd barely moved into the vicinity of his yard when the distinctive click and hiss of sprinkler heads popped up all over the yard. Well, she'd complained about being hot, maybe this was one of those unanswered prayers, because before she could blink she was blasted in the face with cold water.

The sound of laughter rang in her ears as she wiped the water from her eyes and tried to move out of the line of fire. It didn't matter. Every direction was the line of fire.

"Turn them off! Turn them off!" she yelled.

"Well, if it isn't Miss Nosy," Hank said, going back to watering his flowers. "I wondered how long it would take you to make your way over here. Haven't you ever heard that curiosity killed the cat."

"Are you crazy? I'm not nosy. I was just passing by, and I decided to be neighborly. Were you raised in a barn or something? You don't turn the sprinklers on people who are trying to be friendly."

"Lady, you've been watching me out your window for the last six weeks. That's a little more than neighborly if you ask me. I've been sleeping in long johns because I was afraid I'd wake up in the middle of the night and see you peeping through my window."

"Got something to hide, do you?" she smirked.

He turned the water hose toward her.

"Don't you dare." She snarled.

Hank snickered and sprayed her new shoes till they were soaked. She stumbled backward, tripping over one of the sprinkler heads, and landed flat on her back in the grass. Classic cop move. Hit her when she wasn't expecting, like she was a common criminal and drop her to the ground.

Agatha stared straight up, noticing how pretty the canopy of trees was over his yard, and she took a couple of calming breaths. It didn't help. She turned her head to make sure no one had witnessed her embarrassment and then rolled to her hands and knees.

"Sorry," Hank said, his smile saying he was anything but. "My hand slipped."

"Sorry?" she croaked out. "You're sorry?" She mumbled a few choice phrases under her breath.

"You do that a lot, you know?"

Agatha stared at him blankly. Maybe she had brain damage. "What are you talking about?"

"You talk to yourself a lot. I noticed when you were standing back there on the sidewalk trying to decide how to approach me."

"How could you possibly see that?" she asked. "You had your back turned to me the whole time."

He gestured the water hose toward an odd metal disc that hung from the big oak tree. It was obviously lawn art of some kind, different sized circles cut with different designs, and when the wind blew the circles intersected each other. But when the wind wasn't blowing, it made a perfect disc, just like a mirror.

"A tool of my trade," she finally said, deciding not to give him the satisfaction of calling her out. "And I haven't been watching you. That's my office window, and I've been looking out of it since I was a little kid. I like to watch the neighborhood when I'm thinking."

"Well, it's creepy."

"What's creepy is that you're in public wearing that outfit. The only reason you caught me off guard was because I couldn't stop staring at your Birkenstocks. What is this? 1995?"

"And what about that day at the café?" he asked. "I might be retired but I've got ears like a bat. You were sizing me up like a stud at auction."

"Don't flatter yourself," she said, scoffing. "I was sizing you up for my friend. I'm a much better judge of men than she is."

"What'd you decide?" he asked.

"That you've got too much baggage. I told her to run fast and hard in the opposite direction."

"Finally," he said. "The first sense you've shown since you decided to stalk me."

"Sugar, if you think I'm stalking you then maybe you weren't the hotshot cop everyone seems to think you were."

A squirt of water hit her center mass, but this time she charged like a linebacker going in for the tackle. It didn't occur to her that he was twice her size. She was only seeing red.

"Are you crazy, lady?" he asked incredulously. He dropped the hose and put a hand against her forehead so her swings didn't even come close to hitting him.

"I was just trying to be neighborly and introduce myself," she said, panting as she continued to try and reach him. "You big...you big, bully."

She realized he was laughing at her and it made her even more angry.

"Settle down, wild cat," he said, chuckling. "You're the one who came on my property and insulted my shoes. I'm just defending myself. What's wrong with my shoes? They're comfortable."

She took a step back so he was no longer touching her, and they were squared off like two boxers in the ring, waiting to see what the other was going to do next.

"You're scaring the whole neighborhood in that getup. Wearing a gun and Birkenstocks is like a Republican carrying around a Planned Parenthood card."

"Are you on medication?"

"Don't be ridiculous," she said, waving away the accusation. "But it's obvious you're way out of your element. The clothes, overwatering your garden, your Yankee accent."

"I don't have an accent," he said. "You're the one with

the accent. And I'm retired. I'm supposed to do stuff in the garden and wear track suits and do crossword puzzles."

"What are you, forty-five? Give me a break. You're about as ready for retirement as I am."

"I'm fifty-two," he said, stiffly.

"Well, then," she said, rolling her eyes. "You might as well order your casket and check in at the nursing home. You're about the worst retired person I've ever seen. You've got decades left to live."

"Wow, that's depressing. Thanks for ruining my morning."

"Seriously?" Agatha said. She pulled her soaking wet shirt away from her body and stared him down. "Your morning is ruined?"

"Look," he said, putting his hands up in surrender. "Maybe we should start over. I'm Hank Davidson."

"Yeah, I know." She figured at this point she had nothing to lose since she probably looked like a cat that had been given a bath. "One thing you'll find out real quick is that everyone knows everything about everyone in this town. Believe me, even the deepest secrets are hard to keep."

"No offense, but my life depended on keeping secrets. And what I learned was that you can keep secrets if you don't blab them to other people. Even if you tell just one person it's not a secret anymore."

Okay, she thought. Maybe he had a point. Heather had been her best friend since grade school. Of course, *she* knew Agatha's pen name. And when her parents had been alive, she'd of course told them, even though her career hadn't been near as high-profile as it was now. They'd been proud of her. Wouldn't they want to share that with their closest friends?

She sighed, feeling even more defeated. Not only did everyone know who she was, she was still suffering from a major case of writer's block.

"You look like your favorite dog just got run over," he said.

"It's been that kind of week."

"Do you have a name?"

"Agatha," she said.

"Old fashioned," he said. "I like it."

She narrowed her eyes and said, "I can't tell you how relieved I am to hear it."

He grinned and she decided the best thing she could do was forget she ever met Hank Davidson and walk home.

Agatha didn't say another word. She just turned on her heel and started walking. She didn't even care about recruiting him to help her solve her plot dilemma.

"Hey, Aggie," he called out.

She froze in her tracks, feeling her blood pressure come to a boil.

"Don't call me that," she said without turning around. She thought she heard him chuckle and gritted her teeth.

"Nice to meet you, neighbor."

Her one-fingered salute was quick and to the point, and she stomped away to the sound of his laughter.

CHAPTER THREE

"PLEASE TELL me the rumors aren't true," Heather said from their regular booth at the café.

Her white-blonde hair was freshly blown out and her face was expertly contoured. Between her shoes, her handbag, and her jewelry, Agatha was afraid she'd need an armed guard to get out to her car.

"You're going to have to be more specific," Agatha said. "This is Rusty Gun. Babies cut their teeth on rumors."

"Let's see," Heather said. "Where should I start? Maybe I should start with you standing like a drowned kitten in Hank Davidson's yard. Or maybe I should start at the part where you charge him and try to wrestle his gun away from him like a maniac. Or maybe I should start with the fact that you were trying to make a move on my man."

"To be fair," Agatha said. "I wasn't trying to wrestle his gun away from him. And I wasn't trying to steal him. Believe me, you can have him. He's no prince."

"Are you telling me the rest of it is true?" she asked, her mouth open in shock.

"I'm not confirming or denying anything," Agatha said primly.

"A bus full of senior citizens on the way to Shreveport saw you. I don't think you can deny it."

"They're old," she said, shrugging. "What do they know? How come they didn't report that Hank knocked me right on my kiester with his high-powered water hose? He could've seriously injured me. And he called me Aggie."

She took a drink of sweet tea and wished Penny would bring another basket of rolls. She *really* needed carbs for this conversation.

"The jerk," Heather said, supportively. "I'm surprised you didn't shoot him."

"I couldn't shoot a man wearing socks with Birkenstocks. What kind of person would that make me?"

Heather winced sympathetically. "I think that cured me of my infatuation."

It was Wednesday, which meant the special of the day was chicken fried steak and unlimited sides. She was a comfort eater, and it was only by the grace of God, fantastic genetics, and the fact that she ran every morning that kept her from being the size of a house. The way things were going, she was thinking about starting an IV and just feeding herself the cream gravy intravenously.

"Come on, Agatha. What's really going on. I cannot believe you attacked that man on his own property."

"I didn't attack him," she protested. "At least not first. I was just going to introduce myself. We're neighbors and I was jogging right by his house." She was making confetti out of the straw wrapper in front of her. "I thought maybe he could give me a couple of ideas to get my story moving again. I haven't put any good words on the page in more than a week."

"Ahh," Heather said knowingly. "Now the truth comes out. You've been a little high-strung lately. And you're getting a wrinkle between your eyebrows from frowning so much. I told you to come with me to the spa and have a collagen treatment. Marta will get rid of that thing in a hurry."

"It's just, I've worked my tail off for the last ten years. I've lived and breathed writing. I sacrificed for it because I loved it so much. I quit college a semester before graduating."

"Yeah, but that was mostly because of the creepy stalker. It was safer for you to quit and easier for you to hide by retreating into your writing."

Agatha sometimes forgot how perceptive Heather was. She might seem like an airhead piece of fluff, but there was a sharp brain buried in there somewhere.

"Okay, so maybe the stalker had a lot to do with it. But it was still a sacrifice. I always regretted not finishing my degree. I sold shoes for Pete's sake."

"And they weren't even the good shoes," Heather chimed in, looking down at her Jimmy Choos.

"I researched and wrote and researched and wrote. I spent hours and days pouring over crime scenes and talking to cops and immersing myself in that life so I could write books that made people feel as if they were right there on the page. And then the day came that I got published and I thought I'd made it, but I had a choice to make.

"I'd lived for years in seclusion. All because of one man. The fear I had during those years..." Her mouth was dry, so she took a drink of tea. "It was unlike anything I'd ever experienced, and I never want to experience it again. He watched and waited, and I could feel his eyes on me. I knew he'd end up killing me. He almost did."

"That bastard's going to be in jail a long time," Heather said, patting her on the hand.

"I know," Agatha said, attempting to smile. "My point is that what happened to me then affected my whole life. Even my writing. After I got published I could have claimed my own name for my books. You'd be seeing Agatha Harley in big letters in all the airports instead of that stuffy old A.C. Riddle. But it was much easier to sit in my room in mama and daddy's house, in a town that barely warranted a speck on the map, writing my stories and submitting them anonymously. After a while I became that eccentric writer with the mysterious identity, and my publisher decided that helped sales, so now I'll always be anonymous."

"Honey, you've never been anonymous to me or anyone else who's taken the time to get to know you. You're the most special person I know, even if you do have abysmal taste in shoes. And I'm a little worried about you being alone for the rest of your life. Like I've told you before, the heroes in your books don't actually exist. Take it from me, sweetie. I know men. And there's no such animal as the ones you write about."

"No offense Heather, but if you were to throw a dart in a room of a hundred men, you'd hit the worst of the lot. Trust me, there are good men out there. I write about real heroes. The stories I tell might be fiction, but they're based off real cases with real victims. The men and women I write about, they never forget the dead. They carry those memories not just through their careers, but through their whole lives."

Almost as if by fate, the brass bell that hung over the door jingled and Hank Davidson walked in, bold as life. He had the kind of presence that commanded attention, and she and Heather weren't the only ones who'd noticed his arrival. She wanted to think the pounding in her chest and lightheadedness had something to do with the irritation she'd experienced the last time they were in each other's presence, but she had a feeling it had more to do with what he was wearing.

"Good Lord," Heather said. "It's like Archie Bunker and Panama Jack dressed him. What is he wearing? And why is he still so attractive."

"I think he's just really bad at being retired. It's like he's got this image in his mind of what it should look like, but he's clearly in the prime of his life. Retirement is the last thing I think about when I look at him."

"Oh, ho," Heather said, raising her brows. "So that's the way the wind blows, is it? Well, you can have him with my blessing. You were right when you told me he was going to take a lot of work."

"Nope," Agatha said. "Get that dopey look off your face. I'm just having flashbacks from yesterday. I can't decide if I want to rip off those socks or just run out screaming."

Not to mention the fact that she'd spent the better part of her evening the night before researching Hank Davidson. He'd lead some of the biggest criminal investigations in America. He was the best of the best—both revered and hated.

"Well that's your problem, sugar," Heather said. "Socks are not what you should be wanting to rip off that man."

"Hush," Agatha whispered as Hank's gaze met hers. She knew exactly why he'd taken early retirement. And maybe he deserved a little kindness in his life as he adjusted to retirement.

"I'll be back." Agatha scooted out of the padded booth and straightened her blouse. She blew her bangs, which desperately needed a trim, out of her eyes.

"Oh, Lord," Heather said. "This is going to be bad. Please don't embarrass us. And remember that everyone has a camera phone nowadays."

Agatha waved away her concerns and headed toward Hank's table. He always sat at the same one, his chair in the corner so he could see both the kitchen area and the front of the restaurant at the same time. He might as well have been wearing a sign that said, "Cop," on his forehead.

"How's it going neighbor?" she asked, taking the chair across from his.

"Can I help you?" he asked, staring at her blankly.

"Seriously?" she asked. "You don't remember me?"

He squinted and then tilted his head to the side. And then he grinned. "Oh, yeah. How's it going, Aggie? I didn't recognize you dry."

"Hilarious," she said, narrowing her eyes. "But I thought about your suggestion yesterday and agree that we should start over. We are neighbors, after all, and if I'm being honest, I did have a reason to come see you yesterday."

"I know," he said, maddeningly. "I figured there was a reason you had to give yourself a five-minute pep-talk. Why don't you just ask?"

"Because I'm horrible at talking to people other than my close friends," she said.

"You mean like the lady who keeps sticking her head in the aisle to look at us?"

Agatha felt the blood rush into her cheeks. "Yeah, like her. I'm just saying, I'm not exactly social. I mean, I'm fine when I have to interview someone for research, but that's different. It's just asking questions and taking notes. But small talk..." she shrugged. "I'm that person that makes things more awkward." She paused for a few seconds when he just stared at her. "Like now."

He chuckled and then called for Penny to bring tea for both of them. "Unsweet for me," he said."

"Unsweet?" she asked. "You might as well shout to the world that you're a Yankee."

"The sweet tea makes my teeth hurt," he said. "I wasn't here a week before I thought I might end up in a diabetic coma."

"That's funny, because that's how I feel every time I see you wearing socks with those sandals." She couldn't help but snicker as he held up his foot into the aisle.

"Okay," he said, once the drinks were in front of them. "I'll make it less awkward for you. Maybe just ask what you want like you're conducting an interview. What are you?" he asked, narrowing his eyes all of a sudden. "Hopefully, you're not a journalist. I've had my fill of those. You'll have to buy your own sweet tea if that's the case."

She swallowed and felt the nerves inside her. She'd lived her professional life in hiding, never revealing her pen name, even to the cops and medical examiners she'd interviewed over the years. But lately, she'd began to feel the restrictions of her success. And she often wondered if she was really living at all.

"I'm a writer," she said. "A mystery writer to be exact."

"Oh, yeah?" he asked. "You published?

"Nineteen times," she said. "And another due out next month."

"So, what would a mystery writer want with a retired nobody from Philadelphia?"

"Hardly a nobody," she said. "Word on the street is you were a cop."

"Seven months and ten days," he said.

"I beg your pardon?"

"I haven't been a cop in seven months and ten days. I

retired for a reason. I don't know anybody here and nobody knows I'm here, and that's the way I want it to stay."

"So you're hiding?"

The look in his eyes told her not to press further. Fortunately, she didn't need to. That's what the internet was for.

"What do you want, mystery writer?"

"I need help with the book I'm working on."

"No, thanks," he said. "There was nothing I hated more in college than writing term papers."

"I don't need you to actually write the book," she said with exasperation. "I'm just thinking we could maybe help each other. I can imagine that after being a cop, watering roses and doing crossword puzzles is making you stir-crazy."

"You could say that. What do you suggest?"

"All of my books come from real cases. But my current book is a cold case. And no matter how I look at it, I can't figure out the ending. It doesn't make sense, and at this point, making up my own ending seems...unsatisfying."

"Go on," he said, obviously intrigued.

"I've got a sixteen-year-old girl named Nicole Green. Eight years ago she was found on her father's farm, not twenty-miles from here, with her skull smashed in. Not only did the killer sexually assault her, but after delivering the fatal blow he rolled her into a pond and buried her naked body with debris and branches. No arrests were ever made."

"There are thousands of cold cases all over the country," he said. "If you want this one solved your best bet is to talk to the sheriff and see if he has an extra deputy to assign to it."

"I want you," she said.

"I'm retired."

"No, you're hiding. You said so yourself."

"Even more reason to not get involved."

Agatha huffed out a breath in disgust and pulled a couple of bucks out of her pocket. "I'll pay for my own tea anyway," she said. "Sorry to have bothered you."

He grabbed her wrist to stop her before she could scoot out of the booth, but she glared at him and he removed it immediately.

"You never told me the name you write under," he said. "Maybe I'll check out your books since I seem to have so much free time."

Agatha let a litany of names she'd like to call him go through her head before she finally answered.

"You realize you just said all of that out loud," he said, laughter crinkling his eyes. "You swear like a cop."

"I've spent a lot of time with cops. It's always my goal to write them as accurately as possible."

"Lady, no offense, but the only way you could do that was if you were a cop."

Agatha rolled her eyes and scooted out of the booth.

"Are you going to tell me your name or not?" he asked.

"Sure," she said, her irritation obvious. "It's not like you're actually going to read me. The name is A.C. Riddle."

The burst of laughter he let out had everyone in the café looking in their direction, and Agatha felt the blood rush to her cheeks in embarrassment.

"Lady, who are you trying to fool? You are not A.C. Riddle. I've read every one of his books. And that's a man who knows cops. In fact, I'd be willing to bet money he used to be a cop, and that's why he never does appearances. He probably worked under cover."

The embarrassment she'd felt a second ago was replaced with rage. "There's your first mistake," she said. "*He* is a *she*, and that *she* is me. And I'll take that bet. The A.C. stands for Agatha Christy. My first and middle name. Riddle was my mother's maiden name."

She straightened her spine and stood her full height, looking down at him with contempt. "Now, if you'll excuse me. I've got a cold case to solve."

CHAPTER FOUR

HANK HAD to give credit where credit was due. The food in Texas was delicious. And fattening. He'd been eating more than his share of chicken fried steak and barbecue over the last several weeks.

Restaurant choices were limited in Rusty Gun. Other than the Kettle Café, which was where he'd been eating lunch almost every day for the last six weeks, there was Bucky's Brisket Basket, which was only open for dinner and was always crowded. Both restaurants were on the long strip of Main Street. The locals knew if they wanted other options they'd have to drive twenty minutes to the nearest town.

He ate most of his meals alone, but every once in a while, Karl Johnson would come in and join him while he was on his dinner break. Hank missed cops. He missed talking with them and hanging out with them. Even Karl, who was barely wet behind the ears, was a sight for sore eyes.

Karl was a good kid, and more important, he was still

enthusiastic about the job. He didn't have the shade of cynicism that came with every passing year on the job.

"These twelve-hour nights are killing me," Karl said, taking the chair next to him so they both sat facing the door.

"I started my career just like you," Hank said to Karl.

The waitress came to the table, and he pointed to the grilled chicken salad on the menu. Sheila was probably close to his age, maybe a couple of years old. Her black hair was braided intricately, and the wrinkles on her face showed a life of hardship, but when she smiled it lit up the room.

He wasn't sure if she owned the place or if she just acted like she did, but she took care of the employees and the customers with an ease that few could master. Her hands were bare and there was nothing soft about them, and she wore jeans and a t-shirt with the restaurant name in big yellow letters across the front.

Sheila shook her hand and cocked a hand on an ample hip. "Honey, do you smell that? That's the smell of melt in your mouth ribs fresh out of the smoker. Douse 'em in some of our homemade sauce, and *mmmm*," she said, putting her fingers to her lips and kissing them. "Delicious."

"Don't tempt me, Sheila," Hank said. His stomach rumbled, voicing the need for ribs. But his stomach was the problem. It wasn't quite as flat as it had been when he was on the job. "I'm trying to be good. Retirement hasn't been good for my waistline."

"Sugar, you look just fine to me, but I'll get your salad. What about you, baby?" she asked Karl. "Want the usual?"

"Yes, ma'am. You know I'm not going to pass up the ribs."

Karl waited until Sheila had left to give their orders to the kitchen and then said to Hank, "I sometimes think about eating healthier. But what if I get shot in the line of duty? Do I really want my last meal to have been a salad?"

Hank snorted out a laugh. "I used to think that way too, kid. Believe me, age will catch up with you one day."

"You're dreamin' man. I don't know who you're trying to fool about this retirement bull. You're in better shape than every man in here, except for yours truly," Karl said with a cocky grin.

Karl grabbed a hot roll from the basket and broke it open, slathering the inside with butter, and Hank's mouth watered at the smell. Lord, he missed bread.

"What did you mean when you said you started your career just like mine?"

"I started in patrol with Philly PD, and I was humping twelve hour shifts too. But I learned more about police work during those days than any as a detective."

"That's crazy, man," Karl said, shaking his head. "You worked all over the world. Heck, you trained at the FBI Academy. You lived every cops' dream. And you're gonna tell me patrol was better? Pull the other one."

"Variety, Karl. When you go 10-8 you never know what to expect." A 10-8 was active duty. "But when you get that call that all heck's about to break loose, that's when your juices start to flow and everything you've trained for is set in motion. Then it's up to you to create a solution."

Hank took a long swallow of tea, wetting his dry mouth. If the guys could see him now, what would they think of what he'd become? The more he thought about it, the more he realized he didn't really care. Those days were in his past. Retirement didn't mean he was dead, even though that's what he'd thought at first. It just meant he was on a different path. Agatha had been right. He had a whole lot of life to live. He just had to figure out how to live it now that the only thing he'd ever known was gone."

"I love that feeling," Karl said. "Nothing like slapping a pair of cuffs on someone."

"Arresting people isn't always the solution," Hank said.

Karl's excitement dimmed a little. "Sheriff Coil says the same thing."

"Trust your boss. He's a good man."

Sheila brought their food and set it in front of them, and then refilled their tea glasses. Hank thanked her, and then they said grace before eating.

"I know it's none of my business," Karl said after a bit, "but what's going on between you and Agatha Harley? I've noticed there's some tension."

"You and everybody else in town," Hank said rolling his eyes. "Last time I went to the drug store I was asked if spraying neighbors in the face was how they greeted each other up north."

Karl chuckled. "All I'm saying is Agatha is the real deal. She reminds me a lot of you."

"Talk about crazy," Hank said. "How in the world is that woman like me? She's a scatterbrained mystery writer. Even she admits that she's not good in social situations."

"No offense," Karl said. "But I haven't noticed you making a lot of friends around town."

Hanks lips twitched. "I grow on people."

"I'm just saying, outside of Sheriff Coil and the other deputies, y'all are the only two people I trust. I mean, really trust. She thinks like a cop, and she has a heart for the victims like you do. She came to me with this cold case she's working on for her book, and I'm not afraid to admit that you're the most qualified man for the job. She really needs your help."

"I'm not sure what I can do," he said. "I'm a retired cop from up north. No one's going to talk to me down here."

"Good detective work is good detective work, no matter where you are or your status," Karl said. "It's not just about writing a book to her. You'll never hear her talk about herself or her success. In fact, I'm pretty sure she still thinks no one actually knows her pen name around here. She doesn't like publicity. She doesn't seek it. A lot of that has to do with the stalker that terrorized her during college."

"Stalker?" Hank asked. "What happened with that?"

"I don't know all the details," Karl said, shrugging. "But I know she almost died. And I know the man wouldn't have stopped coming after her. He's been in jail for almost two decades, and she's been here hiding."

Just like him, Hank thought, his blood boiling at the thought of what Agatha must have gone through.

"She still lives in her parent's home around the corner from you," Karl said. "Her parents died in a car crash a few years back. There was black ice on the road and an eighteen-wheeler skidded right into them."

Hank winced. "That's rough." He knew what it was like to lose people you loved. How it shaped you forever.

"After they passed away, she could've moved away or built a mansion on the outskirts of town. But she didn't. Have you read her work?"

"Yeah," Hank said, a knot forming in his gut. "Every one of them. I thought the guy writing them was a cop, using his own cases."

"They were all cold cases," Karl said. "Cold cases she helped solve. She does it as much for the victim as she does for the book. She's been a victim, and she knows things could've ended much differently for her."

A voice came through on the Motorola police radio Karl

had set on the table, a mixture of static and garbled directions.

"Shoot," Karl said. He motioned to Sheila for a to-go box and she hurried from around the counter.

"Here you go, baby," Sheila said. "Let me do it for you. I'm faster."

Karl reached for his wallet. "Gotta go," he explained to Hank. "Shoplifter."

"You don't have to explain to me," Hank said. "Put your wallet away. This one's on me."

Karl nodded and bolted toward the door, his to-go bag in hand.

Hank's blood had started pumping the second the radio had sounded. Old habits died hard. Maybe he could be of help to Agatha. It's not like he didn't have the extra time. And she'd piqued his curiosity. He'd been thinking about the case since she'd cornered him that afternoon at the café.

"He's a good kid," Sheila said, cleaning up Karl's side of the table.

"Yes, ma'am," Hank agreed. "But it's a tough business for good kids."

"What kinda kid were you?"

"I just wanted to help," he said for lack of anything better.

"Don't we all, cowboy. Don't we all."

"Put his food on my tab," Hank said, pushing back his empty plate.

Sheila waved him off.

"You're a sweet man, Hank Davidson," she said, and then she laughed. "Don't look so surprised, honey. Sheila knows a good man when she sees one. But this meal is on me."

"Oh, no. I couldn't," he said. "You're not working here for free."

"Sugar, this is my place, and I can do what I want to. It's the least I can do. You've been good to Karl. He never had a daddy, so the time you take to talk with him means more than you'll ever know."

Sheila's eyes watered when she spoke about Karl, and Hank could tell they were close.

"Thank you, Sheila, but it's my pleasure. Really. He's a good man."

"That's the only kind I know how to raise," she said, grinning. "Karl is my youngest. I'm as proud as can be of that boy."

"You've got every reason to be," Hank said. "And thanks for dinner. I'm sure I'll see you tomorrow night." Hank slipped a twenty beneath his plate for a tip, and he realized this was the most he'd enjoyed himself since he'd been in Rusty Gun. Now all he had to do was figure out what to do with Agatha Harley.

He left with a wave goodbye, and he pushed open the glass door that led into a small square foyer. A movement caught his eye, and he froze as a shadowy figure slid to the left of the outside door. He instinctively reached for his weapon, holding it down at his side. In his experience, dark shadows never meant anything but trouble. And just because he'd come to Rusty Gun to retire didn't mean that he couldn't be found.

Instead of taking the risk, he moved back into the restaurant and hurried toward the rear door, through the kitchens.

"Everything all right, Hank?" Sheila asked, concern etched on her features. "You need me to call Karl to come back?"

"It's fine," he told her. "I'm just being cautious."

The truth was, the adrenaline and danger made him feel more alive than he'd felt since he first arrived in Rusty Gun.

The kitchen was chaos in motion. The heat and steam from the smokers, combined with the chatter as the wait staff and cooks issued orders. He held his weapon down and out of sight as he moved through to the big metal door at the back and pushed through. The fresh air was welcome, and he breathed in deeply.

The instant his eyes adjusted to the dark, he moved fast from the back of the building toward the side. The movements were second nature, and he angled his body with weapon aimed ahead. He took small steps, arching from left to right until he was able to see around the corner undetected.

"Bingo," he muttered.

There was a person huddled next to the side of the door, right where he'd seen the shadow pass from the front. He looked around, but didn't see any other threats. Their back was turned to him, clearly expecting him to come out the front. That was their first mistake. He never did the expected.

He steadied his pistol and moved without sound toward his target. The technique known as a cat walk required that he curl his back, bend his knees, and walk with an exaggerated heel to toe rolling step. It was exhausting, but deadly and efficient in moving undetected.

Hank's heart raced and his shoulders burned as if they were holding sandbags straight out in front of his body. The cat walking caused his quadriceps to fire hot nerve impulses through his muscles, demanding his body to relax. His gaze was focused on the target, but his senses were open, listening for other threats.

He wasn't as young as he used to be, but he was mentally tougher than ever. He stopped about ten feet behind the target. It was a safe cushion of space in the event his target turned to attack. The bullet would travel just as fast from ten feet as it would at five. He stood, making himself as erect as possible, giving off an imposing silhouette on the wall.

"You looking for me?" he asked, his voice menacing and low. The gun steady in his hand.

The figured jumped at the sounds of his voice and they turned with a gasp.

"Holy cow," Agatha said, staring wide-eyed at the gun. "First you shoot me with the water hose and now you have a gun aimed at me. I'm going to have to draw the line with this one. Have you ever considered anger management classes?"

He narrowed his eyes and muttered under his breath. "Aggie," he said, putting away his gun. "What a surprise."

CHAPTER FIVE

"I CAN'T BELIEVE you were prepared to shoot me," Agatha said incredulously.

"If you're not prepared to shoot, there's no use carrying a gun," Hank said. "You were the one skulking around like a common criminal. If you don't want to be treated like a perp, then don't act like one."

"I was just waiting for you to finish up your supper. I was being polite. It's Main Street for Pete's sake. It's not like I was hiding behind a dumpster waiting to jump out at you."

Hank sighed. Maybe she had a point. "You're right. I apologize."

"And you're forgiven," she said, smiling at him. "Now that we've gotten that out of the way we can get down to business."

"Have you eaten?" he asked. "It seems the least I can do is buy you dinner."

"Have you noticed we both spend an inordinate amount of time in restaurants?"

"I don't cook," he said.

"Me either." Agatha looked up at the sign for Bucky's

Brisket Basket. "Might as well eat here. The smell of those ribs is sinful."

Hank sighed, wondering how much temptation he was going to have to stand for one night. He could feel his salad mocking him. He opened the door for her and they maneuvered their way to the table he'd just vacated. Sheila had just gotten it cleaned off.

"That was fast," Sheila said. "And look, you brought back a friend. Hey, Miss Agatha. How you doin', girl?"

"I'm starving," she said. "Bring on the ribs."

Shelia chuckled. "You got it. And maybe you can talk your fella here into sharing with you. I know that lettuce must be gnawing at his insides by now."

Hank knew a losing battle when he saw one. He could always eat better tomorrow. And if he was going to sin a little he might as well do it all the way. He grabbed a roll as soon as Sheila put them on the table.

"So, why the change of heart?" Agatha asked him.

"Let's just say I suck at being retired. My plants are overwatered, I've fed the birds so much they just flop their fat bodies around the back yard, and I've done all the expert level crosswords in my book. Besides, someone intervened on your behalf and stated your case convincingly."

"Karl," she said, matter of factly. "I took the case to him on your advice, but he told me he didn't even know where to start. There was a reason the case went cold. They've got no other leads."

"There's always something," Hank said. "It just needs fresh eyes."

"Exactly," Agatha said, smiling at him. "I knew you'd understand."

He hadn't really taken the time to look at her. He'd seen her, of course, but he hadn't taken the time to see more than the soaking wet, slip of a woman with the smart mouth. And now that he'd *seen* her, he wished he hadn't looked. She was...interesting. Her excitement shone in every expression on her face. Her eyes were an interesting shade of bluish green, framed by dark lashes, and when they weren't spitting fire, they were filled with good humor and intelligence.

Her hair was pulled back in a ponytail and there was a smattering of freckles across the bridge of her nose. Good grief, how old was she? It was impossible to link the books he'd read by A.C. Riddle to this woman. The books were filled with a depth of understanding that no one of her age could grasp.

"How old are you, anyway?" he asked.

"You know you're never supposed to ask a lady that question," she said, biting into her bread. "I'm thirty-eight. But if you ask me that in another two years I'm going to lie."

Okay, so she wasn't as young as he thought she was.

"I look younger, right?" she asked, grinning. "I have a theory about that."

His lips twitched. "I'm sure you do."

"I think it's because I've never been married. I've got friends ten years younger who've only been married a couple of years, and they look like they've got one foot in the grave."

"Interesting theory. I can see why you're not married." Hank smirked.

"I'm married to my job. Getting into the heads of killers is much more exciting."

"That's what you think."

"You're married?" she asked.

Hank cursed silently. He'd opened himself up for that one.

"No," he said, curtly.

She looked a little taken aback at his tone, but he wanted to make it clear that wasn't a subject open for discussion. He had to give her credit. She went on as if nothing happened.

"Most people just think I'm a crazy cat lady who has an obsession with online shopping. I get a ton of boxes delivered to my house. Or maybe they think I'm a drug dealer. Either way, it gives me a mysterious presence."

"You've got cats?" Hank asked.

"No, I'm allergic, but why ruin the image?"

Sheila delivered a platter full of ribs to the table. Enough to feed a whole family. And he realized they hadn't ordered. He guessed there was no need for it.

Agatha inhaled appreciatively, and he wasn't sure he'd ever seen a woman get that look on her face over a plate of ribs.

"So," she said. "You ready to feel alive again?"

"I'm bored. Anything to shake the dust."

"Good," she said. "If this relationship is going to work we have to be a team. I'm not a rookie when it comes to this stuff, and you're retired. We're equals who both have something to offer. Which means I'd better not get any more shots of water to the face or guns pulled on me. I've got a conceal to carry permit. You don't see me pulling out my gun and waving it in your face every time you put your foot in your mouth, now do you?"

"I'm going to pretend you didn't just insult me," he said. "And I'm still on the fence about you being armed. At least until I know you can shoot that thing."

"I'll try to remember to keep both eyes open," she said deadpan.

He would've laughed, but he wasn't quite sure if she was serious or not.

"This is a murder case," she said. "And it's sat in a file cabinet for the last eight years. That girl deserves justice."

"They all do," he said soberly.

"We don't have to follow the same rules the cops do. When it's time to be a cop, use that to our advantage. But sometimes these things take a little...imagination."

"Aggie, I know how to work a murder investigation, and I've been known to bend the rules from time to time. But I'll never dishonor the badge by breaking them."

"Good, that's what I was hoping you'd say."

"Well then," he said. "I guess that makes us partners."

"I know you were a cop," she said. "That's easy enough to read all over you. But when you say you know how to work a murder investigation..."

He could see the guilt on her face, and he was starting to enjoy himself. She thought if she could get him to tell her about his career then that would let her off the hook for snooping.

"Aggie, let's go ahead and pretend that you already know the answers to all that since you've probably used your considerable resources to find out as much as you could about me."

Her cheeks turned red and she dropped her gaze, choosing to focus on her ribs.

"Look, if we are going to work together we have to trust each other. But just as important as trust is respect. Let's leave the cat and mouse for the crooks." He held out his hand in a truce.

"You've got a deal," she said, placing her hand in his and gripping tightly. "Partners."

CHAPTER SIX

THURSDAY MORNING COULDN'T COME EARLY ENOUGH for Agatha. She decided to skip the morning walk because she was meeting Hank at the café for seven-thirty. This wasn't her first start on a new case, but it was her first time working with a partner.

It was May in Texas, which meant the temperature could variate to thirty degrees in a single day. She opted for jeans and a sleeveless shirt, and grabbed a cardigan to ward off the morning chill.

Cold cases might've seemed less intense because the leads, emotions and sense of urgency had faded, but it was just the opposite. While there may not have been a corpse on scene any longer, the emotions associated with not catching the killer grew stronger with each passing year. The families became angrier—more bitter.

Agatha had also learned during her research that law enforcement detectives grew overly proprietary with the cases they couldn't solve. Simply put, they took it personal. It was not unusual for a police department to welcome her unjaded eye to give a new perspective to an old case, but the actual detective assigned to the case was nothing less than openly hostile and non-receptive to her being involved in what they deemed as their case.

Agatha arrived at the cafe, and as expected, Penny was already on shift. Agatha looked around the cafe and noticed there were very few people inside. Most folks didn't go to work in Rusty Gun till eight or nine o'clock, so there was no need wasting the precious thirty minutes mulling around downtown when they could catch another half hour of snooze time. The people in her hometown lived a laidback way of life she'd always appreciated.

Agatha noticed the man in the far corner booth immediately. His hair was slicked to one side, and his face was shaved smooth. The steam from his coffee wafted from his mug to partially conceal the deep cleft in his granite chin. She knew it was Hank sitting there, but what she couldn't figure out was why he was dressed in a pin-stripe Brooks Brother's suit.

"Oh boy, did I underdress for the occasion," she mumbled.

She stopped herself. Considering what he'd been wearing since he moved to Rusty Gun, the suit was a definite upgrade. He stood when she approached and she could see a liveliness in him that she hadn't seen before. He needed this as much as she needed him.

"Wow," Agatha said, looking him over from head to toe. She still couldn't believe he was fifty-two. The man knew how to fill out a suit. She was a professional, but she wasn't dead.

Hank immediately began to ask questions about the crime. Agatha knew a natural pecking order wasn't established the night before, but would be crucial, or otherwise she'd end up as his assistant running errands and getting coffee. It wasn't that she couldn't stand up for herself as much as it was his sheer force of will that was hard to say no to.

"I think it's best we take it slow to start as we build our relationship together," she suggested.

Agatha liked the way partner sounded as long as he didn't mean assistant.

"Working together is going to take a little practice. I've never had a partner, and from the research I've done, you like to work alone"

Agatha spoke firm and held onto the case files even though Hank had stretched across the table once for them. Hank nodded. They'd both have to be willing to sacrifice to each other to get what they wanted for themselves.

"Equals," he said, holding out his hand again.

She handed him the files just as Penny came up to refill his coffee and ask her what she wanted for breakfast.

"What are you having?" she asked Hank.

"Oatmeal and wheat toast."

Agatha wrinkled her nose in response. "Nevermind. I forgot you hate food. I'll have the pancake breakfast, Penny. Eggs scrambled. Make sure there's gluten in my pancakes. That's the good stuff."

"I don't know how you stay so skinny," Penny said, writing down her order. "If I ate like you I'd be the size of a house."

Penny headed back to the kitchen.

"I hope your roses don't suffer now that you have something to fill your time," she said.

"My roses will be fine. I hired a gardener, and I've been instructed never to touch them again."

Agatha relaxed. It usually took her a lot longer to feel

comfortable around people. But there was something about Hank that put her right at ease.

"Let's get the dirty details out of the way before we go any farther."

Agatha stared at him, completely confused. "Dirty details?"

"I'm a consultant. You need me for my level of expertise. I'd assume you're used to doing this with people. You know too much not to have had consultants help you out before. How are you compensating me?"

"Oh, right," she said. "I've hired plenty of consultants before." She'd actually brought her standard contract, but for some reason, she'd thought that Hank wouldn't need one. That the love of the case would be enough for him. She guessed she was wrong.

"I brought a contract with me. I'd never expect you to work for free, but you'll need to sign the non-disclosure agreement along with the contract. I think you'll find the fee and expenses are satisfactory."

Hank eased a pair of black, plastic framed cheater readers from his breast pocket. The contrast between the glasses and his salt and peppered hair completely changed his appearance. He was a modern-day Clark Kent.

"Why the NDA?"

"Because my book ideas are my intellectual property and they're sold on proposal. Even though this is a cold case I don't want someone else hurrying to write the same book to beat me to the release date. It basically says you can't say anything about what we do or discover."

"Okay," he said, signing. He slid it back to Agatha and then his expression changed.

"What's wrong?" Agatha asked.

"We're not exactly equal partners now, are we? Just because you're paying me doesn't mean I work for you."

Agatha hated to break it to him, but it kind of meant he did work for her.

"Let's just say when we're working the case that we make decisions together. When it comes to the finances and expenses though, I'm calling the shots. Fair enough?"

"More than," he said. "Now tell me about our victim. What's her name?"

"Nicole Green," Agatha said.

"It's always important to give them a name. The victims are never just faceless, nameless beings. Just because it makes it easier on us to treat them that way doesn't mean it's the right thing to do."

"I know," she said. "I see them in my dreams. They speak to me. And what we do to bring them justice and let them rest in peace never seems like it's enough."

Agatha grabbed a clump of napkins from the metal dispenser and wiped the table dry. Then she hefted her briefcase from the seat next to her onto the tabletop, turning each wheel of the combination lock and then snapping open the clasps.

"This is what I've been able to get hold of from internet and public records searches. It's not much, but it's a start."

Hank slid each page around, putting them in a straight line in front of him, until they began to show a pattern of reporting and chronology. Agatha picked up on what he was doing and felt the warm satisfaction of knowing she'd made the right choice in partners.

"This is more than a good start," he finally said. "There've been many times all I had to go on was an anonymous phone call or tip written on a torn napkin."

"Nicole was sixteen-years-old and attended Bell

County Preparatory School. She and her father lived in the unincorporated portion of Bell County. It's about a twenty-minute drive from here. There's good news and bad news," she said.

"What's the good news?"

"Your pal Sheriff Coil has jurisdiction."

"And what's the bad news," he asked.

"Your pal Sheriff Coil has jurisdiction and he's a might touchy about the case since it went unsolved."

"I've known Sheriff Coil a lot of years. He's a great cop and a good man. Maybe you should give him the benefit of the doubt."

"Look, I realize he's your friend, but you can lay off the intimidation tactics," she said, straightening her spine. "I'm speaking the truth. He might be a great cop and a good man, but the facts remain that this case is unsolved and it was his responsibility to solve it. And the fact also remains that he doesn't seem too thrilled about getting new information or having someone else look into it."

"I promise you that Coil wants this case solved more than anyone. Cops stick together, Aggie."

"I've noticed," she said, raising a brow. "Maybe that's part of the problem."

"What's that supposed to mean?"

"I mean that you and Coil are friends. If he's got nothing to hide and wants this case solved, then he should be open to talking to you about it and getting you whatever information you need."

Agatha stacked all the files and put them back in the briefcase.

"What, are you taking your toys and going home?" Hank asked.

"No, I'm avoiding the morning rush and curious eyes.

We can take this back up at my house. Believe me, the gossip mill is already having a field day because we're having breakfast together. When they find out why, the poop is going to hit the fan. Everyone here remembers Nicole Green's murder, and everyone is more than aware that there's probably a murderer living amongst us."

"The poop is going to hit the fan?" Hank asked, laughing. "I think your name has you stuck in another era."

"Good manners are timeless," she said haughtily.

"Good point."

CHAPTER SEVEN

HANK HAD ADMIRED Agatha's house, even before he knew it belonged to her. It looked like a storybook cottage. It was gray stone with diamond-paned windows, and ivy grew riotously along the stone. It was small, but two-stories, and the front door was arched and painted bright red. It was a house that looked like it belonged to a creative person.

He'd followed her home after they'd left the café, and he'd parked his car in his driveway and walked down the street to her corner house. The temperature was rising, and he was thinking maybe the suit wasn't the best idea. It was only May and the temperature was already hotter than what he was used to in Philadelphia. He couldn't imagine what it would be like in the next couple of months.

He took off his suit jacket and loosened his tie. Agatha was already at the red door, putting her key in the lock. He noticed the cameras immediately, one at each corner of the house, along with spotlights. There were also cameras beneath the eaves near the door, so whoever was on the porch could be seen from the front and the back.

"That's a lot of cameras," he said, as she motioned him

inside. The shrill beep of an alarm countdown greeted them and Agatha quickly typed in her code.

She grinned at him. "Those are just the ones you can see. It would be a bad idea to try and break in this place."

He liked the inside of the house immediately, and he thought about what Karl had told him. Agatha could be living in a mansion somewhere, but instead she chose her childhood home. Comfortable was the first word that came to mind. The floors were wood and polished to a gleam, and the staircase was narrow and led straight up to the second floor.

The front of the house was tidy and there was the lingering smell of lemons, as if it had been cleaned recently. There was a sitting area to the left with a couch and two chairs positioned in front of a fireplace, and on the right was a room with a piano.

She led him past an open kitchen and breakfast area that had obviously been remodeled. The back of the house was all windows that looked out over a back yard that could have been a park, with big towering trees and a pergola with a porch swing.

The room just off the kitchen and breakfast room was clearly meant to be the family room, but Agatha had turned the entire space into her office. He guessed it made sense, considering the amount of time she must spend working.

"Ignore the mess," she said.

"It's kind of hard to do that. I don't ever think I've seen this much of a mess."

"It's my work space. Creativity doesn't necessarily lend itself to order."

"Then I guess I'm glad I'm not creative."

"It's organized chaos. I know where everything is. I promise."

An entire wall was lined with bookshelves, but the books weren't lined like the ones in his office. Some were stacked, some were upright, and papers seemed to stick out of all of them. It was driving him crazy, and the urge to straighten them was strong.

The other wall had a white board that stretched from one side to the other, just like in a classroom, and it was filled with notes in black marker that looked like barely legible scribbles. A huge monitor sat on one side of the L-shaped desk along with a fancy ergonomic keyboard. A laptop sat next to it. On the other side was a set of table shelves filled with bobbleheads. She had everything from Gandalf to Sherlock Holmes.

"Interesting company," he said.

"It's good to have someone to talk to when I've got plot problems."

"Hmm," he said, starting to reconsider what he'd gotten into. Maybe his first impression of her the day she come traipsing onto his lawn had been the right one. Maybe she was just nuts.

His attention went to the board with crime scene photos. They were graphic and brutal in their starkness, and it reminded him of the investigative war rooms he'd spent so much time in during his career.

"This is a heck of a setup. Other than the mess."

"What, you thought I sat around in my pajamas all day to write?"

"Do you?"

She grinned. "Usually. There's a reason I run every morning and eat out most of the time. It forces me to get dressed and leave the house."

"Can we agree on one thing before we go over the murder board?" Agatha asked.

"Sure, what?"

"That no matter where this investigation takes us, we'll let the facts and the reports speak for themselves?"

"I'm not sure what that means," he said, confused. "Are we back to talking about Coil?"

"Not exactly."

"What you have to understand that in most cold cases, the facts are usually skewed and the reports are usually shoddy. I can't agree to limit our work to that," he said.

"I guess what I'm saying is that if Sheriff Coil did a crap job, then we should acknowledge it and do a better one."

Hank's muscles tensed. Coil was one of his closest friends. He was the reason Hank picked Rusty Gun for his relocation. He didn't know what Agatha had against Coil, but it was starting to get on his nerves.

"Fine," he said, just to get things moving. "Where's the board?"

Agatha stared at him a few seconds, as if she was debating whether or not to say more, but wisely, she stayed silent.

She grabbed a remote from the desk and clicked a button, and automatic blackout shades lowered on all the windows. She clicked again and the dry erase boards slid open and then rotated back into the wall. In their place came an electronic dry erase board and a Prometheus board. Two overhead projectors lowered from the ceiling.

"Holy crap," Hank said.

"You like? I've got to spend my money on something. The house might be old, but I can promise everything is the latest in technology. The whole house runs on voice activated commands when I want it to. The security system would make you cry if you knew all of its capabilities."

"It's like the Bat Cave"

"Look at you! You know comic books. You didn't seem like the type."

"Everybody knows Batman. What do you mean I don't seem like the type?"

She crinkled her nose, and he'd started to recognize it as a habit of her thinking something she might not want to say out loud.

"You just seem very...proper," she finally said. "You've got the suit. And then there's the way you arrange your trash."

"What's wrong with the way I arrange my trash?"

"Nothing," she said, rolling her eyes. "I'm sure it really helps the garbage men a lot to organize everything like that. You put your recyclables in the bin all neat and orderly, your cardboards are precisely the same size, and your beer bottles make a cute little pyramid."

"Have you been going through my trash?"

"Of course not," she said, waving away the question. "I'm very observant, and I run right by it on my morning jogs. Now, if you're done with the interrogation, maybe we can get back to work."

Hank raised his brows, amused at how she'd turned the tables on him.

"I don't drink coffee," she said, "but I've got a stocked Keurig in the kitchen, so help yourself."

"You don't drink coffee?" he asked. "At all?"

"Nope. Disgusting stuff. Smells nice though. I live on tea. Here's the box," she said, lifting the box of information she'd received from the sheriff's office onto the desk. "You can make yourself comfortable and start going through it."

"Right," he said. Hank looked for a place to hang his jacket and finally decided to lay it over the back of a chair, along with his tie. He unbuttoned his top button, rolled up his sleeves, and decided to take her words of making himself at home to heart, so he headed for the Keurig to make himself a cup of coffee.

"Sugar is in the bowl next to the Keurig," she called out. "Milk is in the fridge."

Hank grunted in appreciation and then brought his cup back to her office area. She was at her desk, already absorbed in whatever she was reading. She had a long table, like a mini-conference table, that divided the room from the kitchen and breakfast area. She really did have everything they needed, and more. He grabbed the box, surprised at how light it was, and then took a seat in a straight-back chair at the table. He always worked best in a straight-back chair.

Hank opened the box and the first document sitting atop a scattering of other papers was the Bell County Sheriff's Office report filed by the first deputy on scene. He lifted the single page report up by his thumb and forefinger and frowned. Then he started to read and he understood what she meant when she'd told him it was less than exemplary police work. He couldn't dispute that.

"This is it?" he asked. "A half-written report?"

"Yep. It's a big box with a whole lot of air in it. I've got the crime scene and autopsy photos I can put up on screen when you need them."

"I'm good for now. What we need is facts. And I'm not getting them from this thing," he said, dropping the single sheet of paper back into the box. "You're going to have to fill in the gaps for me."

Agatha flipped the projector on so images came on the screen, and she lowered the lights halfway.

"Like I told you before. We've got a sixteen-year-old girl who attended a private prep school. Tuition isn't cheap for that place, but Nicole was there on full scholarship. She was a bright kid, and pretty in an understated way. Her home life was rough. Mom died young, and she was left to be raised by her father. And let's just say he's not exactly someone you'd want to spend a lot of quality time with. He's a farmer by trade, but not a successful one. Mostly he drinks.

"The medical examiner ruled Nicole Green's death as a homicide. COD was blunt force trauma to the left temporal bone."

The autopsy photos came up on the screen, and Hank studied the head wound intently.

"The skull was shattered with such force that shards of bone were found in the brain. She wouldn't have survived even if medical personnel was standing right there."

"Any signs of sexual assault?" Hank asked.

"She was sexually active. They interviewed the boyfriend during the investigation. He said they'd been having sex about three months, and he admitted that he'd seen her and they'd had sex around the time she disappeared, but his alibi held up. But the ME's report said she'd had sex just prior to her death."

"Anything else they failed to follow up on?"

"Oh, and she was pregnant." She added

"How come none of that's in the police report?" Hank asked, looking into the box again in case he missed something.

"Don't know. The only reason I know that much is because I started asking questions. And it's not like my source is exactly reliable. George Mayfield was a deputy during that time, right at the end of his career. He retired the next year, and then a couple of years after that was diagnosed with Alzheimer's. The man could remember every detail of every case he ever worked. Except he couldn't remember names."

"Those aren't exactly hard facts," Hank said.

"No, but it's what we've got. The ME didn't find anything to dispute that she was having anything more than consensual sex. There was no vaginal bruising, no skin under the fingernails, no bites or scratches. Nothing to indicate assault pre-mortem other than the killing blow."

Hank moved closer to the pictures and whistled softly under his breath while he was thinking.

"What about post-mortem?"

"Plenty of those. She was killed on her property, on a small hill that overlooks a pond. It's an overgrown area. Lots of hackberry trees and tall grass. Whoever gave her the blow to the head rolled her down the hill and tried to conceal her body in the pond. She's got a bunch of post-mortem scratches."

"So the questions are, what was she doing there and who was she with? Was the murder weapon ever found?"

Agatha shook her head, "Nope. But the ME report suggests the victim was probably waist-high when the blow was struck. Maybe on her knees. The weapon's trajectory was slightly downward, but across. Like swinging a baseball bat." She demonstrated the swing.

"So the boyfriend is alibied. Maybe she's seeing someone on the side? The place you're describing doesn't exactly sound like a romantic oasis. It's a place you go because you want to hide. To keep a secret. So Nicole meets up with this mystery boy, has sex, and then when she's getting up, he clocks her over the head with something like a baseball bat."

"And that brings us nicely to my next point," Agatha said. "Some of the kids at school said that Nicole was seeing someone else. That she had some secret boyfriend, but none of them knew his name. And it just so happens, Nicole's father, Walter, said one of his field workers disappeared around the same time."

"You know what they say about coincidences," Hank said. "Who's the one who suggested Nicole and the field worker were seeing each other?"

"Walter Green," she said. "Like I told you, a few of her friends at school said she was supposedly dating some older guy, but they'd never met him and didn't really care to."

"What did the boyfriend have to say about that?"

"He said he'd heard the rumors, but didn't believe them. Apparently, there was quite a mean girls club at that school, and Nicole was often the target."

"Was Walter able to give the police information on the field hand? Were they able to track him down?"

"Nope. Said he was a transient. After they both went missing, Walter said he just assumed Nicole had run off with him."

Hank pursed his lips in thought. "How long was she missing?"

"Twenty-eight hours."

"And Walter dismissed her that quickly?"

"He wasn't exactly a doting father. I'm surprised he realized she was gone at all. The only reason he did was probably because his supper wasn't on the table that night."

Agatha sighed and leaned back in her chair, staring at the screens and the pictures there. "Nicole was a nice girl, but she wasn't popular. She was a poor farm girl going to a school with the kids of congressmen and pro-athletes. Her uniforms were hand-me-downs, and she drove an old pickup truck. According to George Mayfield, the boyfriend said the other girls were jealous of Nicole. She was beautiful and smart, and apparently the boyfriend was pretty popular. This made the mean girls even meaner. According to what little is in the report, these girls started so many rumors about Nicole that investigators were chasing false leads left and right.

"I want to know more about the father. Walter Green. How could he have hired this boy as a farm hand and not even know his name?"

Agatha shrugged. "It's common out here. Transients, hobos, and ranch hands come and go."

"How did Walter know the guy would come back to work each day?"

"They get paid in cash at the end of the work day. George said they looked long and hard at Walter Green, but they came up empty."

"Has the field hand ever identified or found?"

"No."

"Was an area search conducted for him?" Hank pressed.

"I just said he's never been found."

"I mean did they look for his body," Hank said.

"Oh, I have no idea. I haven't seen anything like that in any of the reports. And George didn't mention it."

"Do you think we can we gain access to the crime scene?"

Agatha laughed. "Let's just say I lost a shoe out there a few weeks ago. I was lucky I didn't lose my life."

Hank's eyes narrowed. "What happened?"

"Walter Green didn't appreciate the fact I was trying to find his daughter's killer. He ran me off with his combine tractor and a few rounds from his rifle. I've never been so scared in my life. And I really liked those shoes."

"I doubt Coil would be able to get a search warrant for the area unless we come up with some new evidence."

"I've got a drone," Agatha said. "That's what I used to take the current pics I have of the crime scene, but after eight years, the field hand's body would be buried under so much muck and debris that it would be impossible to see anything from the air. That's if the animals left us anything to see to begin with."

Hank knew she had a point. "We've got to find another way to identify the field hand."

"How?" Agatha asked.

"Nicole was sixteen. Sure, she was surrounded by mean girls. But girls that age have someone they can confide in. There's always that one girl who sticks to the fringe of the popular crowd because she doesn't want to become ostracized, but she doesn't participate. Nicole would seek that girl out. They would be best friends."

Agatha put a photograph on the screen. It was a group of twelve girls, and Nicole was on the end. It was a stark contrast to the autopsy photos he'd been looking at before.

"It's a shame," Agatha said with a sigh. "She was a beautiful girl with her whole life ahead of her, but she was a tortured soul on so many levels. These are the girls from what would have been her graduating class. Eight years ago. These girls would be finished with college now and beginning to make their nasty marks on the world.

"I know some of these girls. A couple of them are from Rusty Gun. The girl on the other end, that's Rhonda Mitchell. She was part of a big scandal the following year. She had to drop thanks to an unexpected pregnancy."

"Teenage pregnancy isn't all that uncommon where I'm from."

"Where, around here, when a local youth pastor knocks up a minor, it gets a little bit of attention."

Hank's eyes widened at that information, and then he looked at the picture again and the girl Nicole was standing next to. They had their arms around each other and their smiles were bright.

"This one," Hank said. "She was Nicole's confidant. We need to find her."

Agatha's fingers flew across her keyboard. "She's already found. Sheena Walker."

"You know, Aggie, as far as partners go. You're not bad. How'd a writer end up having the instincts of a cop?

"It's a long story, but the short version is I always wanted to be a writer, but when I went to college I didn't really know what I wanted to do with myself. I didn't want to be an English major or get a creative writing degree. So I decided the best thing I could do was get a degree where I could use the information I learned in my books. So I majored in forensic anthropology.

"It was exactly what I needed. I started writing about the crimes we studied in classes, and things went from there. I was so focused on my writing I actually quit school the semester before I was supposed to graduate. Fortunately, my first novel sold not long after.

"I've been all over America researching cases. I helped solve some of the most notorious cold cases. But this one has given me nothing but trouble."

"In that case, it's a good thing you hired me," Hank said. "Let's go talk to Sheena Walker."

CHAPTER EIGHT

AGATHA MADE a sharp right and hit the accelerator, speeding down I-35 in her Jeep Wrangler.

"I think this is a quicker route," she said.

"I think you left part of your muffler back there at that turn," Hank said.

"Nah, this baby was made for off-roading. You need to relax. I know these roads like the back of my hand. It's time to loosen up, Davidson. You're in Texas now."

"Is it always this hot?" Hank asked.

Agatha laughed. "Hot? It's only May. This isn't hot."

She noticed he'd buttoned his shirt back up and put on his coat. He must be sweltering. His hair was damp at the temples, so she turned the A/C up to full blast.

Most of Rusty Gun was within walking distance. It was basically just one main street and a grid of fourteen blocks in each direction. But the unincorporated areas spread things out a bit. Bell County was expansive, yet sparsely populated.

Rusty Gun had been a main passage point along the famous Chisholm Trail, but they'd lost the bid to the neighboring town of Salado to build a bridge in the 1800s. Neither town ever saw much growth after that, as railroads bypassed each town to the north and south.

Sheena Walker had been Nicole Green's friend, and they were hoping she could tell them some new information. Maybe something she'd remembered after so many years. Sheena worked at the Bell County Commissioners Livestock Auction and Trade Association, and they figured that was the best place to pin her down. They were out in the middle of nowhere.

The old Jeep bounced when Agatha exited the interstate for a dirt service road before making a sweeping left and curling back to the right for a giant, empty gravel parking lot. The land was vast and there were several metal barns and fenced areas where different auctions took place. Despite the location, the parking lot was crowded.

The gravel crunched beneath her tires and she spotted the empty parking spot on the front row. "Look at that," she said. "It's fate."

"Or maybe everyone is terrified of your driving and decided to get out while they still can."

She blew him a raspberry, but couldn't help but grin. "It's a good omen."

There was a big sign and sidewalk that led up to the largest barn. It was completely enclosed, and she waited while Hank opened the door for her. A chime signaled and an artic blast greeted them.

"Lord, that feels good," he said.

There was a reception area where those who were participating in the auctions could pay and get a number. And there was a long plate glass window where they could see into a large arena. It smelled of livestock and hay.

"Bless you," Agatha said as Hank sneezed. And then she said it again. "You going to be okay?"

"I will be once we get out of here," he said. "Look, there's Sheena." Then he sneezed again.

Sheena approached. She was early twenties and several inches shorter than Agatha. Her skin was beautiful and smooth, the color of dark chocolate, and her smile was radiant. She wore jeans and a button-down work shirt with a pair of boots.

"Sheena? Hank asked, extending his hand.

"Yes, sir," she said, taking his hand and shaking. "How can I help you?"

"Do you mind if we have a word? In private?"

"Are you with the state commission?" She asked, a look of concern on her face.

"No, are you expecting them?" Agatha asked, "We'll be quick."

"No," she said. "I just saw that fancy suit and figured you had to be from somewhere official. Why don't you come back to my office and we can take a few minutes? Where did you say you were from again?"

Her office was right in the front and glassed in so she could see everything happening from all sides. There were two chairs in front of her desk and a couple of pictures of her and her husband, one on their wedding day and another more casual at the park. Their smiles were beaming in both of them.

"We're actually here about a friend of yours," he said. "Nicole Green?"

Agatha knew the technique he was using. The best way to get a read on people was to surprise them with certain information. It often revealed more about the person they were interviewing than they wanted.

Sheena's knees buckled and she grabbed on to the edge of her desk, and she dropped into her chair. Her eyes were wide and there was hope in them.

"Have you found him? The person who killed her?" she asked, her voice hoarse.

"No," Hank said. "I'm sorry. But we're hoping to. We've reopened the investigation."

Sheena nodded. "She was my best friend."

"That's why we're here. We're hoping you've remembered something over the years. Maybe something you didn't mention the first time around."

"Her death still haunts me," she said, shaking her head sadly. "She deserves some peace. Poor thing never had peace her whole life. Maybe she can now that she's dead."

"The only thing that's going to put this to an end is the truth," he said.

Sheena nodded. "There were so many lies the first time around. All I can remember is the chaos and confusion. The gossip was out of control. None of it helped anyone. We all went our separate ways after graduation. I haven't talked to them since then, though I see some of them on Facebook from time to time.

"Are you talking about these girls?" he asked.

"Yes. Can you believe they didn't even attend her funeral service? What a group, huh? They were friends to your face and then they'd stab you in the back before you could even turn around. They were horrible to Nicole. But Nicole...she kept coming back for more. It was all she had. She said even bad attention was better than she usually got. Her daddy was horrible. I think he was abusive, but she'd never say. And then she hooked up with Ty and you'd have thought she found her ticket to salvation. Nicole was looking for someone to take her off of that farm.

I don't think she cared who it was with as long as it was far away."

"I need to ask you a few questions," Hank said. "I'll apologize now because they might bring up painful memories, and I'll also stop the moment you say enough. Okay?"

"Okay," Sheena said, her voice monotone.

"You and Nicole were close?" Hank asked.

"Like sisters," she said. "She was the poorest girl at school and I was the only black girl at school. We had a lot in common as we were both outsiders. My mama and daddy have more money than most of the families that attended, but it didn't matter. They only saw what they wanted to see."

"You said you thought her dad was abusive," Hank said. "What made you say that?"

"Just little things. She'd never let me come to the house. She'd have bruises on her upper arms and sometimes her neck. They looked like fingerprints. You could tell she was scared of him. She spent as much time away from home as she could. It was amazing her grades were so good.

"I know the church tried to help her. She spent a lot of time there. I think she was praying for a better life. She said it was the only place she ever really felt true love."

"Who gave her the hardest time?"

"Oh, gosh. They all did. Connie would tease her about her hand-me-down clothes. Georganne would steal her textbooks so she couldn't study, or rip up her homework. Michelle was constantly making plays for her boyfriend, touching him and sending him notes so Nicole could see.

"How about Rhonda Mitchell?" Hank asked.

"I forgot about her. She left school after she got pregnant and I never saw her again."

"It seems everyone knew about her pregnancy."

Sheena snorted out a laugh. "Rhonda got herself full of what we like to call the unholy ghost. The youth pastor had a thing for teenage girls. We all heard the rumors, but no one ever had proof and none of the girls would ever rat him out. At least not until Rhonda became pregnant."

"Did she and Nicole attend the same church?" He asked.

"Sure, almost everyone went to First Methodist."

"You knew Nicole was involved with someone else, didn't you?" Hank asked. "Someone she shouldn't have been?"

Sheena's mouth dropped open in surprise and she started to shake her head.

"Nicole is dead, Sheena. Keeping her secrets isn't helping her anymore. We need to know who she was seeing."

"I don't know," she said.

"Please, Nicole."

"I don't know his name. I swear. But he was older, and she talked about how much he loved her and how special he made her feel. She said Ty had the money, but this guy had her heart. I think Rhonda found out about them. She was furious with Nicole about something. I saw them arguing. And she was brutal to Nicole from that moment on. I think Rhonda could have killed her. She was that angry."

"Do you think Nicole was having sex with the same youth pastor that got Rhonda pregnant?"

Tears trickled from the corner of Sheena's eyes. "All I can do is suspect. I don't know. She said they'd have sex after church, so it was someone there. She was scared to death her daddy was going to find out. She said he'd kill them both if he ever did. And then they found her body and she was gone forever."

Agatha reached out and squeezed Sheena's hand, and she handed her a tissue.

"I'm sorry, Sheena," Agatha said. "I know how hard this must be for you."

Hank held up his phone and said, "I've got to take this call. Can you finish this up?" Agatha nodded, wondering what he was playing at. His phone hadn't been ringing.

Agatha cleared her throat. "Do you know for a fact Walter Green killed Nicole?"

"No. It's just what everyone said. But it makes sense. He was so awful."

Agatha didn't bother to let her know that he hadn't changed much over the years.

"What about the guy that worked for Walter? The man that disappeared the same time that Nicole was killed? Do you know who he is?"

Sheena's brow creased in thought. "I've got no idea."

"Do you think he could have been the older man Nicole told you about?"

"I don't think so," Sheena said. "I saw that guy around a couple of times. The thing you've got to know about Nicole was she had a certain idea of what a guy should look like."

"I don't understand," Agatha said.

"I'm just saying Ty was smokin' hot. He was the hottest guy in school. And Nicole said the other guy was even better looking than Ty. A real man, she called him. Said he even had a couple of tattoos."

"Was the youth pastor up to Nicole's standards?"

"I mean, don't get me wrong. He was hot. But he was probably close to forty. He was just so old. I don't see how she could've been attracted to him.

Agatha's mouth pressed tight so she wouldn't say anything to correct Sheena's misconceptions about age.

"What about Rhonda? Did she have the baby?"

Sheena blew out a breath and winced. "Oh, she had the baby. But you can imagine the reception she had. Especially in our circles. Her parents disowned her. She was going to run off with the youth pastor, but he left town in the middle of the night. When the law finally caught up to him he'd already founded a cowboy church up in Wyoming. He had a new name and was doing the same kinds of things to the girls there. He ended up getting caught up there, and that's when Sheriff Coil was able to get him brought back to Texas to stand trial. Rhonda took the baby to the courthouse every day, but the trial didn't last long. He got life in prison."

"The youth pastor is in prison? A local prison?" she asked excitedly.

"They sent him off around Palestine," Sheena said. "It was in all the news."

"You've been a big help, Sheena."

She couldn't wait to tell Hank. This was the first news she'd gotten on this case since she'd started it. Maybe Hank Davidson was her good luck charm.

"Do you remember the youth pastor's name?"

"Jim, or James. I don't remember a last name."

"That's okay. We can look him up in the prison's directory."

Sheena gripped her hand and shook her head. "You can't go to the prison."

"We won't mention your name. I promise."

"It's not that," Sheena said. "You know what they do to child molesters in prison?"

"Shoot," Agatha said, a sinking feeling in her gut. "They killed him, didn't they?"

"He didn't even last two days."

CHAPTER NINE

THE ELATION and adrenaline of finding out new information wore off almost as soon as they'd gotten it. The drive back to Rusty Gun was made in silence, and Agatha turned off the alarm and kicked off her shoes by the door.

"You want some tea?" she asked Hank.

"Sure. I'm going to run home and get out of this suit. It smells like bull crap. Literally. Give me a few minutes, and I'll be back." He shut the door behind him and headed down the street to his house.

Agatha walked back into her office and dropped onto the chaise she had in front of her bookshelves. It was her favorite place to read. It was also a good place to nap. Her head was pounding. Too much excitement and too little payout.

Agatha had zero interest in continuing the investigation that afternoon. It would be best to start fresh the next morning, when she didn't have someone drilling spikes in her head. She had a feeling interviewing Rhonda was going to take energy.

Her cell phone buzzed and the screen lit up. It was Heather.

"Hello," Agatha said.

"Was that Hank Davidson I just saw leaving your house? Girl, you've got some serious explaining to do. I don't know what you told him to get him out of those ugly socks, but I want to hear all the details."

"We're working."

"Lady, I just happened to be driving by when Hank came strolling out of your house. He looked worn out, so good job."

"Where are you?" Agatha asked, looking into her back yard. She almost yelped when Heather's face appeared in the window.

"Good grief, what are you doing?"

"I'm trying to see if Hammerin' Hank earned his reputation. Girl, you look like something the cat dragged in. You need to close these blinds if you're just going to do it out in the open like that."

"I'm not used to having people standing on my back porch staring in. You're a very creepy friend."

"That's what my second husband always used to say."

"Hank's helping me with a case for my book. That's it. I'm not even going to invite you in because I have a screaming headache, and I think my eyeballs are in danger of falling out. In fact, I'm going to close my eyes now."

"No wonder," Heather said. "Why don't you rest a bit, and then you can meet me downtown for margaritas."

"Sounds good. I'll meet you at seven." Agatha hung up the phone and immediately dozed off.

"Aggie. Hey Aggie."

Hank's voice was like a bee buzzing in her ear. Agatha cracked her eyes open, but squinted as the afternoon sun hit them. She could hear someone moving around in the house and the cold chill of fear gripped her. She was disoriented, and her head was still pounding.

She rolled to her side and quietly opened the wooden box that was sitting on her bookshelf, and then she pulled out the revolver her dad had left her.

"Aggie, are you in here?" the voice said again. "It's me, Hank."

She released the hammer of the Colt .357 and exhaled in relief.

"I'm in here," she said. She sat up, but immediately pressed a hand to her temple.

"You okay?" Hank asked, coming to her side. "Here, let me take that." He placed the revolver back on the bookshelf. "I was only gone about fifteen minutes. Did something happen?"

"My head is pounding," she said. "I think this case is getting to me more than it should. I keep thinking about that youth pastor. What kind of person does it make me that I'm glad he's dead. After what he did to all those girls."

"I wish I could tell you," he said, his voice gruff. "But I feel the same way. Some things you don't question. Vengeance belongs to God. Sometimes He strikes quickly."

"I saw Heather lurking about. She said y'all were going out for margaritas later."

"It's up in the air. I don't even think I can stand up right now my head is hurting so bad."

"Why don't you go back to sleep, and I'll take the papers and reports back home with me? I need to be less irritated over the shoddy reporting and more focused on what they did put in there."

"Take whatever you need. Or you're welcome to stay here and use all the equipment. However you're most comfortable."

"I'll take them back. I'm going to pick up some dinner and then settle into my favorite reading chair for the night. I'll see you bright and early in the morning." He picked up the files and loaded everything into the box. "Oh, and if you do go out with Heather, take it easy on the salt. It's bad for you."

Agatha gave him a thumb's up and dropped back down on the chaise. "Thanks, partner."

Hank took a sip of his tea and set it on the table next to his Lay-Z-Boy recliner. He'd caved to the tempting smells at Bucky's Brisket Basket once again. That was two nights in a row. The evidence of his treachery sat next to his cup, a graveyard of bones and sauce. It had been delicious.

He licked his fingers one more time before he started handling the papers. He'd forgotten to ask who the fourth deputy was in this area. The sheriff's office had a couple of satellite offices because of the size of the county and because the land they had to cover was too spread for just one office to handle. The sheriff and four deputies ran things from the office in Rusty Gun. There were four more deputies who worked out of the satellite office in Boot Lick.

Coil had introduced him to deputies Karl Johnson and Maria Rodriguez. And he'd met Deputy Joe Springer at the post office one morning. Coil had mentioned the fourth deputy briefly, as he'd been out recently with appendicitis, but Hank couldn't remember his name.

He grabbed his laptop and searched the Bell County Sheriff's Office Facebook page. The social media posts gave a lot more information than a static website, so it didn't take long to find who he was looking for—Deputy Tyler Gunn.

Hank knew Coil was Sheriff eight years ago when Nicole was killed, and he knew that Maria was his most senior deputy with almost twenty years. So, since neither Karl nor Tyler were there when Nicole's murder occurred, they were off the hook for the cruddy reporting. George Mayfield, the retired deputy with Alzheimer's was also off the hook, as he wasn't the lead officer.

"Man, Coil, I know you're better than this," he said, disappointed in his friend for allowing that kind of work to be turned in.

He settled back and pulled out the report that had upset him so much earlier that morning. It was a few pages shy of being a sticky note. The initial deputy on scene documented the names of the two young boys who found Nicole's body as they sought out a fishing hole. Hank jotted the boys' names down as contacts to speak with later. They'd both been ten at the time, so they'd be adults now.

The report only described where the body was and not where the body may have come from. Was she killed in the water or relocated there? If relocated, then the killer had to have touched her to move her. The report said the deputy notified Sheriff Coil and Lieutenant Tom Earls, who was the senior deputy at that time. Hank had heard a while back that Earls had passed away from cancer.

Hank thumped the report back into the box and fished for Earl's report. Hank smiled as he lifted the report. He recognized the thickness of it. That meant lots of information, and the potential for lots of answers.

"Now we're talking old-school reporting." Hank sighed as he dug into the facts.

An hour passed before he realized he needed a break. He'd become so engrossed in the details that he'd lost track of time. He laughed at the changes in his body now that he'd eclipsed the half-century mark. He was still in great shape, but things changed, and he wouldn't be in great shape if he kept chowing down on rib baskets.

He shuffled throughout his house and made sure all the outside lights were on and the blinds were closed. A chill of awareness snaked up his spine, and he was itching to get back to the report. He knew he was missing something.

Hank skipped on refilling his tea and hurried back to the chair, and he checked his cell phone to make sure he hadn't missed a call from Aggie. There were no missed calls. No one ever called since he'd retired. He sighed. He did miss the constant demands of the job. Phone calls, emails or text messages had blown up his phone day and night. His cell phone service carrier must have thought he was nuts, but the truth was, when you're at the tip of the spear for catching killers, you're also in high demand.

"What are you missing?" he asked. He tossed his reading glasses onto the table next to the empty plate.

It was his second pass through and that old viper of uncertainty had his gut in knots. Lieutenant Earl's reporting was meticulous, with the exception of a few spelling and grammar errors.

Hank set the document down on the foot of the elevated recliner and laid back to allow the facts of the case run through his mind. Being tense never helped him. A relaxed Hank was an intuitive Hank, so he tried to find comfort in the quiet. His mind was on overdrive as the old adrenaline of the hunt had been reignited by the day's investigation, but he knew it was introspection that solved cases.

Experienced detectives didn't get off on car chases and gun fights. That was best left to the young SWAT jocks. No, the old bulls get their kicks by following the details and picking apart facts like a buzzard over road kill. He decided to take a nap to rest his mind. It was only around eight-thirty, so it wasn't like he was burning the midnight oil.

"Siri, set alarm for twenty minutes."

Hammerin' Hank, your alarm has been set for twenty minutes.

He grinned. It was the little things in life that brought pleasure.

CHAPTER TEN

HANK WAITED FOR THE BEEP, and found himself more irritated every time he heard it.

"Aggie, it's Hank," he said. "Call me back. No, never mind the call, just get here quick." It was the third message he'd left in as many minutes. Agatha's headache must've gone away, because when he went back over to check on her the Jeep was gone and the house was locked up tight.

Big revelations in old cases didn't come often. It was usually the result of slow, methodical reexaminations. This was like a smack in the face. There was no time to wait.

Hank paced in front of his window and peeked through his blinds every time he saw headlights on the street. Impatience swarmed inside him and he fought the urge to get in his car and track her down. She was ten minutes away at the Taco and Waffle Restaurant. But she should've answered. A good partner was always on call and ready.

"Forget it. I should've known better than to partner with a wannabe cop that doesn't have enough to do in her life and too much money."

His doorbell rang and he picked up his pistol before

heading to the door. He cracked it open and his left foot remained as a backstop behind the door. He kept his pistol down at his side.

"It's about time," he said, letting her in. He closed and locked the door behind her quickly.

Agatha looked a heck of a lot better than she had the last time he'd seen her. Tacos and margaritas had that effect on most folks.

"You feeling better?" he asked.

"Sleep helped. And the Tylenol. I just needed to clear my head for the evening."

"You been drinking?"

"I had half a margarita. I didn't want to chance it. When I saw you calling I was anxious to get back, so I left Heather to her margaritas and a potential future husband. What was so important? You didn't even give me a chance to answer before you called and left another message. You know that's not how phone tag is supposed to work, right? You've got to give a person the chance to tag back."

"I think I found something," he said. "Come in the living room."

He went to his recliner and grabbed the papers off the footrest. He was in his sock feet and slid a couple of feet as he headed toward the dining room, but he kept his balance.

"Enough with the suspense," she said. "What is it?"

He tossed the file onto the table, and watched as Agatha opened it. She ran a thumb between the first and second pages and he waited quietly as she examined it. But she sat down in frustration.

"What am I looking at?"

"Look closer," he said.

"I've been looking at these files for weeks. I've practically memorized the pages. I'm not seeing anything new."

"Let me see if I can help."

"Just so we're clear," she said. "Your condescending tone makes me want to punch you in the face."

His lips twitched. "Duly noted."

Hank pulled out two more files from the Bell County Sheriff's Office. He pointed to the bottom right corner of each stack of papers.

"Every deputy or crime scene attendant has to fill out a report. These forms are identical," he said, showing her the different reports. "They all have the sheriff's office logo at the top. They all have signatures on the bottom from whoever wrote the report. But what do you see on this document?" he asked.

"Page one of six," she said, reading where his finger was pointed.

"Right," he said, flipping to the next page. "And this one?"

"Page one of fourteen. I'm assuming you have a point to make?"

"My point is every official document from the sheriff's office is the same. Logo heading, signature at the bottom...and numerical page numbers." Hank opened up Lieutenant Earl's file and spread the pages before her. "Now look at these."

Agatha gasped. "There's no numbering."

"Yes ma'am," he said. "A fresh perspective always helps me."

"I will shoot you in the foot."

"What did I say?" He grinned.

"I'm just in that mood."

"You're feisty," he said. "I like that quality in you, Aggie."

"If you keep calling me Aggie I'll shoot you in the face."

He barked out a laugh. "To be fair, it's one of those things that's easy to look over. It doesn't matter how many times you see it."

"You saw it," she said.

"I've been trained to look for the things that are easy to miss. You'd agree that the sheriff's office isn't exactly flush with cash, right?" Hank asked.

"They've been trying to get a tax passed for the last couple of years for weapons and body armor. They do what they can with what they've got. Sheriff Coil has been wanting to hire more deputies for years, but there isn't the money for it." She said.

"You know a lot for an eccentric writer who spends most of her time in her house."

"I like to stay informed on the issues. That's why it's important we vote. It's important our voice is heard."

"All right, Susan B. Anthony. Here's the million-dollar question. Why would an agency that has no extra money waste printer ink making a copy of the original file, then make a copy of the copy before giving it to you. Those copy machine printer cartridges are expensive."

"I guess I'm not following how a wasteful print and copy practice is going to solve a murder."

"At first I thought redacted or scratched out names might have shown through on the first copy, but there is nothing redacted or filtered. Then I realized that a first run was printed so the page numbers could be cut off from the bottom of the report.

"They couldn't give you sliced pages with missing information or you'd become suspicious, so after they cut the page numbers off the copy they copied them again."

Agatha flipped to the last page, "But why the last page?

Even without the numbering, it still has the deputy and Sheriff Coil's signatures on it.

"Something was removed and replaced." Hank waved the paper over his head, "But the question is what. How did you get these files?"

She dug around in the box and handed him a form. "I submitted a Freedom of Information request to Sheriff Coil," she said. "Actually, Sheriff Coil offered to give me the originals, but in my line of work I've learned to cover myself legally and civilly. I'd already had the request prepared and signed, so I handed it to him to keep it all above board. He said he'd have his secretary copy the whole file and to come back the next day and get it."

Hank took the receipt from her. "Your request for information was made March eighth, but your receipt for taking the copies wasn't until March eleventh. Did you come back the next day like he said?"

"Yeah, but it wasn't ready. Coil's secretary said their copier was older than the Alamo and that she'd get the file to me as quick as she could get the thing up and running again. She even dropped it by the house for me so I wouldn't have to make another trip."

"I've never met her."

"Kim Lee," Agatha said with an affectionate smile. "She's been the secretary for the last several sheriffs. Since they're so short of staff she fills in as the day time dispatcher, records clerk, and even part-time bailiff for Wednesday afternoon court."

"She sounds like a heck of a woman."

"I don't know what the Sheriff's Office would do without her," she said. "So what do we do now?"

"I think it's obvious." Hank said.

"I hate to bring this up, but what if it's Coil who

doctored up these reports and gave them to Mrs. Kim to pass along?"

Hank already had the idea, and the thought of Coil tampering set his temper on edge. It would be foolish to overlook the obvious, even if Coil was his best friend. There wasn't a doubt in his mind that Coil was innocent. But even though his heart said one thing, his training told him another.

"I'll handle it," he snapped.

Agatha's eyes widened. "You sure?"

"I said I'd handle it. I think it's best that you go now."

"I thought we were partners?"

"Not this time. Coil won't talk if you're there. This is between me and him."

CHAPTER ELEVEN

THERE WAS no point in putting off the inevitable. That's why he called Coil and asked if he could meet him. Fortunately, Coil was a workaholic and still at the office.

"Hey, man," Hank said, shaking his friend's hand. "Thanks for meeting me so late."

"Anything for you, brother. Sorry our schedules keep conflicting. I've been wanting to get together the last couple of weeks. Now that you're living here, there's no excuse not to. Man, we used to have some good times."

Hank smiled, but it was forced. He felt sick to his stomach.

"How's retired life?"

"It's different," Hank said, sitting across from Coil's desk.

Coil laughed. "That's what I hear. Word on the street is you and Agatha Harley have been spending some time together."

"Word on the street?" Hank asked amused.

"Small streets," Coil said, grinning. "Word travels fast."

Coil was a modern-day cowboy. He was Hollywood

handsome in a rugged way. His boots were scuffed and his jeans faded. He wore a short-sleeve plaid button up shirt that looked like it'd been designed for him. His favorite weathered Stetson balanced on a short file cabinet. In the weeks Hank had been living in Bell County he'd learned one important thing. The people loved Reggie Coil.

"You glad you came?" Coil asked.

"I don't know," Hank answered honestly. "I'm not sure why I'm here. Other than I had no place else to go."

"We go back a long ways. I don't know how many years it's been since we first met at the FBI Academy, but I'm glad we got stuck as roommates."

"Me too. I'm no good at retirement," he confessed.

"That's an understatement. I heard from a bus full of senior citizens that you were out watering roses in nothing but your pistol."

"I had on socks too," he said deadpan. "I'm going crazy in small town. It's so boring. How do you stand it?"

"It's what you make of it," Coil said. It's a safe town. There's not two or three murders a day, and you're not getting shot at. And when that's not your norm you think life's boring."

"The risk is what makes me feel alive." Hank sucked in a breath between clenched teeth.

"Ahh, I see. You feel vulnerable here."

Hank thought it over for a second. "Maybe. I'm out here alone. You're the only person I know. And I'm well aware of the fact that I'm known by certain individuals in certain circles. And I know that my past could come back to haunt me. I'm used to having a team at my back."

"It's an adjustment period," Coil said. "Give it some time. I know from experience. I thought I'd go nuts after leaving Austin for here. But I discovered there's all kinds of thrills in small towns. You gotta know where to look."

"Maybe so. I think I'm feeling a bit too exposed. Like no one has my back. You know?" The tension in his muscles increased the longer he waited. He knew he needed to get to the point.

Coil dug into the back pocket of his tattered blue jeans and pulled out a Sheriff's badge.

"You want to talk about not having back up, Hank? I got three other hired guns working with me. Good deputies, yet we got nothing but land and lakes with no one to watch our six but the good Lord."

"I get your point, Coil."

"Somehow, Hank, I'm feeling responsible for your moving out here, and since you're here I haven't had time to hang out. That's my fault and I apologize. I could've made the transition easier for you."

"I made the decision to come here and then made it permanent by buying a house. Don't worry, I still think you're a good friend although you never helped me unpack."

"Well, that's a relief," Coil said, laughing. "But let's get together for dinner at least once a week. And I'm always up for a beer or two on the weekends."

"That's a deal."

"And if you get too bored, you could always go back on the job. I could put in a good word for you at Austin PD. It'd be a short commute for you."

"You know the truth. I can never go back."

"I know. I suppose that's what's got you feeling so isolated. It's not that you can't stay here. It's that you can't go back there."

"There comes a time when you have to decide if you

need to save everyone else, or save yourself."

"No one knows the horrible stuff we see, so never feel like you owe anyone an apology for walking away. Losing your mind or putting a bullet into it wasn't the answer. Sometimes the brave thing is walking away."

Hank nodded. He knew it was the truth, and there could be no regrets now that the decision had been made. "Sometimes I wonder if I pushed too hard. Drug my mind into wars that my soul wasn't prepared to fight."

Coil tucked his overly long hair back behind his ears. His smile was easy.

"You can't ask yourself those questions, Hank. They'll send you over the edge. After the nightmare I lived in the Austin drug task force, I never thought I'd return to law enforcement, much less a normal life. It was by God's grace that I recovered from that gun battle, but not without a struggle. One thing I learned was to never ask myself if I pushed too hard. War isn't for the weak. Whether it's fought on land or in the mind, it's going to take its toll."

"You're right," Hank said. "Man, I sure wish I had that beer right now."

"I figured you'd eventually get to the reason you're paying me a visit tonight."

"I've agreed to help Agatha Harley with the Nicole Green cold case."

Coil propped his boots on the edge of the desk.

"What have you gotten yourself into, Hank?"

"Should I tell her I can't help her?" Hank asked, wondering if his friend would steer him away from the case. His answer would tell him everything he needed to know.

"No, of course not. If anyone can solve that case, you can. And I've never once heard anyone say anything bad about Agatha. She's weird, but everyone likes her. In fact, the only bad thing I can say about her is she has questionable taste in friends. That Heather is a real nut job."

"I've noticed," Hank said, chuckling. "Can you do me a favor as long as I'm here?"

"If it's legal," Coil said, grinning.

"Agatha accidently shredded Lieutenant Earls' case report. Do you think I could grab a fresh copy?"

"Sure thing," Coil said.

Hank was instantly relieved. Whatever was going on, Coil hadn't been part of it.

"On second thought," Coil said. "Would you mind if I have my secretary print you a copy in the morning?"

A knot twisted in Hank's gut, but he kept his tone even. "I should've just waited and come in the daytime to ask her, but I know how busy she is. I thought I'd save her the trouble. Plus, I'm anxious to look at something besides the news."

Coil stood in front of the locked file room, as if he were blocking the entrance, and then he sighed. "You're right. I was just being lazy. She's got more than enough work to do. Let me grab it for you in here."

When Coil turned his back, Hank grabbed onto the edge of the desk to steady himself. His knees had turned to jelly at the thought of a possible faceoff with his friend.

A moment later, Coil came back with the original case file and tried to hand it to him. Hank raised his hands in surrender.

"Whoa, no way, buddy," he said. "This is the original. I'm not walking out with it. I'll take a copy, but not this."

"Have it your way, but you'll have to wait. I have no idea what the code for the copier is. I haven't made a copy in years. Please take the original. I insist."

"I'll take good care of it," Hank said, taking the file.

"I know you will. I trust you with my life, brother."

Hank quickly thumbed through the file to make sure Lieutenant Earls' report was included. It was, and so were the numbers at the bottom of every page.

"Please don't let Agatha get this anywhere near her shredder." Coil kidded.

"As long as you don't let your secretary know I have the original. I hear she's a stickler for the rules."

"It's a deal," he said, and they shook on it.

CHAPTER TWELVE

THERE WAS something about routine that Hank appreciated. He started every morning the same way. On this Friday, he grabbed a banana and an Ensure and then took them out to the wrought-iron bench in his backyard to enjoy the quiet and the sunrise.

He enjoyed his backyard. The canopy of trees and the chirping of birds. A wind chime tinkled softly from his back porch. This was what retired people were supposed to do. They were supposed to drink their Ensure and watch the grass grow. He wasn't particularly good at relaxing, but he'd trained himself to relax in this place.

It was too early to call Agatha. She usually didn't start her run until seven, and that was at least another hour. Maybe if he sent her a text. He wanted to wait for her to compare the files.

He texted her that he had the original case file in his possession, but he wasn't expecting an immediate response. He should have known better.

Agatha surprised him with a quick text response: *Good*

morning, neighbor. You have the case file? I have coffee. Come over.

He didn't have to be told twice. He showered and shaved and thought about what Agatha had said about his attire, so he opted for a pair of jeans and a white button-down shirt as a compromise. He didn't own a pair of boots—though he figured he should get some at some point—so he put on a pair of loafers and concealed his weapon beneath his shirt.

About thirty-minutes later, Hank was at Agatha's door. She had it open before he could knock.

"What took you so long? How'd you get the file? Did you break into the file room?"

"Slow down, tiger. Nothing as exciting as that. Coil gave me the file. I told you he was a good man."

"But you had to make sure," she said.

He nodded. "But I had to make sure."

"Come in," she said, tugging on his arm excitedly and closing the door behind him. "I can't believe he let you have the original file."

She handed him a cup of coffee fixed just the way he liked it.

"Thanks," he said, surprised.

"Don't get used to it," she said. "So now what do we do?"

"We scan it and get it back to him. Coil is sharp. Once he starts thinking about it he's going to wonder if we've found something. Especially once we start asking questions about his office."

"I've got an automated scanner. It'll take a while, but we still need to go talk to Rhonda Mitchell. It'll be done by the time we get back." Agatha straightened the pages and put them in the tray. "I already have the copied file uploaded into the database. Once this original is scanned the computer can analyze both reports and show us what's different between them."

Hank wasn't a fan of being a passenger, so he insisted on driving to Rhonda Mitchell's house. She lived in Salado and it was a much farther drive. Agatha's Jeep wasn't exactly his style. She seemed like a Jeep person. A person who liked to have the windows down and her teeth rattled. He wasn't that person. He liked comfort. And he liked the fact that his ears didn't ring when he got out of his BMW X5.

"This is nice," she said. "Seems like you. Very safe."

His eyes narrowed. "When you say stuff like that I feel like you're really calling me boring."

"No, of course not. You're Hammerin' Hank Davidson. What could be boring about you?"

"I'll have you know that I've never had a boring day in my life. I've had criminals confess everything they know at the sight of me."

"That's nice, Hank. Turn right up here."

Hank gritted his teeth and stepped down on the accelerator. He wasn't boring and he wasn't safe. He was just retired.

Rhonda Mitchell lived about as far to the west of Salado as she could, without living beyond the town's incorporated limits. Rhonda was reported to be living with her fourth husband on the property attached to her second husband's home. She'd won it in the divorce settlement, and refused to move. Rhonda reminded Agatha a whole lot of Heather.

Or maybe not.

The double-wide trailer sat right at the top of a small hill. On the hill next to it was a mansion that had to belong to the second husband, so he got the pleasure of looking out of his window every day at Rhonda.

From the file Agatha had read, there were more than a couple of daddies for her five children. The police had been called a dozen or so times for domestic reasons, but it wasn't clear if the domestic problem was Rhonda, her husband, or one of her ex-husbands.

Rhonda had gotten a pretty hefty settlement from the church when the youth pastor had been convicted, but it hadn't lasted long.

Gravel crunched beneath the BMW's tires, and then it gave way to a different sound when he eased off the main road and onto the muddy path toward the trailer.

Hank parked behind an orange Camaro, and they looked at each other uneasily as the sound of barking dogs came from somewhere. And then the dogs came into view.

"Holy cow," Agatha said. "That's a lot of dogs. Do you remember Cujo?"

"Yep. I've got just enough bullets to shoot them all."

"If you don't miss."

"I never miss."

The door of the trailer opened and a woman came out, her bathrobe hanging off one shoulder and a cigarette hanging out of her mouth. She narrowed a gaze a Hank's BMW and came toward them.

"Y'all get," she said, shooing the dogs. "Go on now, you worthless things."

Rhonda hadn't aged well. She was twenty-four going on a hard fifty. She was carrying about thirty extra pounds around the middle, and years of smoking had lined her face with premature wrinkles. Her hair was spikey and bleached blonde from a bottle, but she was in serious need of a root touch up.

"What y'all want?" she asked, coming right up to Hank's window. "You from the church?"

Hank lowered the window an inch. "We'd like to talk to you about the tragic loss of your first child's father. I understand things have been difficult for you."

Hank spoke in a hushed tone so she'd have to lean in closer to the car. He also wanted her to shush the three dogs yapping at her heels.

"Y'all shut up and get out of here," Rhonda yelled at the dogs. They scattered and Hank relaxed.

"Geez, I thought she was talking to us," Agatha whispered.

"You a reporter?" Rhonda asked. "I don't want no part of being on TV. Not unless you're paying me. A girl's got to make a living. Why don't y'all come on in and we'll talk about it?"

Hank looked at Agatha and could see she was anxious about running into the dogs again. He wasn't so keen on running into them himself. But they opened the car doors and stepped out onto the soggy ground.

"We'll just talk outside if you don't mind," Agatha said, eyeing the trailer. "I've been feeling a bit under the weather."

"Mmhmm," Rhonda said. "I thought so. I know a pregnant woman when I see one. It's the morning sickness."

"Ummm," Agatha said.

Hank stifled a laugh, and decided to step in before Agatha hurt Rhonda. "We're not here about TV. We're investigators working the case of your husband's death."

She snorted out a laugh. "We wasn't married. That goldarned lawman drug him off to the prison before he could make an honest woman out of me. Then he went and got himself shanked with a shiv. Good thing it didn't disqualify me for a lawsuit settlement from the church. My baby needed that money."

"I can only imagine how hard it must've been for you," Agatha said.

Hank knew she was trying to play on the woman's emotions, but she wasn't doing such a great job of it. The look of disgust on Agatha's face was noticeable. Fortunately, Rhonda didn't notice because she'd been given the opening she needed to tell her story.

"It sure was," Rhonda said. "I don't know how me and little bit survived. That man took everything from me. I could've been somebody. But he was selfish and greedy, and he went and got himself caught with those other girls."

Rhonda looked down at her phone, ignoring them for a couple of minutes.

"Are you waiting on a call, Rhonda?" Hank asked.

"No, I'm playing *Words With Friends*, and it's my turn."

"Sounds fun. I'm sure you have lots of friends," Agatha said, taking the opening.

"Yeah, people are naturally drawn to me. It's how I've snagged four husbands. I should've stuck with number two. He was loaded. But I do miss my Jim. Nobody loved me like he did."

"I bet your friends were jealous of your relationship with the pastor," Agatha said.

Rhonda hmmphed and said, "Of course they were. They were jealous of anything one of us had that the other didn't. We all secretly hated each other. But it was better to keep our enemies close, if you know what I'm saying."

"Sure do, girlfriend." Agatha spurred her on.

"My Jim was special. He had a gift to reach girls in need. Girls like me. But I was his special angel. That's what he told me. I wasn't supposed to worry about the other girls he was trying to heal because I was his true love."

Hank felt a pang of sympathy for the girl, and it just reinforced his belief that justice had been served to Jim in prison.

"And then those men came and tried to take Jim away, and I tried my best to protect him. To tell them it was okay what he was doing. But those other girls had it in for him. Jim told me that the world of evil would come against our special love. He was right."

"I admire a woman who is willing to stand up and fight for her man," Agatha said. "Even if that meant fighting friends who were supposed to have your back."

Agatha had connected with Rhonda immediately, so Hank stood back and let her handle it.

"I've always said it was us against the world. I don't care what the court says. It ain't nobody's business what we do when we're naked."

Agatha swallowed and her eyes were as big as saucers. Rhonda really did belong on a reality show.

"Do you mind if we sit in your nice yard chairs?" Agatha asked. "I need to ask you some real important questions."

"How much you gonna pay me?"

Agatha dug in her purse and came up with a twenty.

"That's a start," Rhonda said, snatching the twenty and shoving it into her bra. "Have a seat."

Agatha sat in the pink plastic lawn chair and Rhonda took the green one next to it. Hank leaned against the hood of the car.

"What you wanna ask?" Rhonda said.

"Do you think it's possible any of the other girls loved Jim like you did?"

"Oh, sure. They all did. How could they not. He was so gentle and kind."

"What about Jim? Do you think he loved anyone besides you?"

Rhonda stared at a space just beyond Agatha's head. She was a damaged woman. Far past the point of repair.

"He loved Jesus," she said.

"What about Nicole Green? Did he love her?"

Rhonda exploded from the chair, knocking it backward. "What are you talking about? Who told you that? That evil little witch is a liar and a slut. I'm glad she's dead. My Jim said she was just making stuff up because she was jealous of us."

"I don't mean to upset you," Agatha said. "I believe you."

"You do?"

"Of course, I do." Agatha pulled out another twenty and gave it to her. "But I need to talk about Nicole for a minute. Did you know Nicole was pregnant too?"

"I...well...maybe she was. But who cares? That wasn't my Jim's baby. It was Ty's. He loved her, but she kept rejecting him because she wanted what Jim and I had. But my Jim was just trying to heal her."

"Ty loved her?" Agatha asked quietly.

"Oh yes. More than anything in high school. Even more than 4-H."

"Do you think Ty knew about Jim and Nicole?"

"Of course he knew," she said, a hardness coming into her eyes that made Agatha shiver.

"How did he know?" she asked.

"Ty was my friend. Of course I had to tell him. But he didn't understand what they were doing. That it was innocent."

"Exactly what did you tell Ty?"

"I might have let it slip where Jim and Nicole were planning to meet. Jim told me he was going to explain to her that she had to stop loving him the way I did."

Rhonda's voice switched to a distant, child-like cadence. Agatha knew her mind had reverted to the past. Rhonda was stuck in a cycle of trauma, loss and guilt. And Agatha knew it wouldn't be long before she shut down completely.

"Did Ty find her?"

Rhonda buried her face in her open hands. Sobs shook her body. Hank stepped in at that point and handed her a handkerchief.

"Rhonda, you're a good mom," he said soothingly, "And we know you have a big heart when it comes to love and looking out for your friends. You're the protector of your family and you tried to safeguard Jim and Ty."

Rhonda sniffled and said, "Yeah, I was always having to take care of everybody else. Who was there to take care of me?"

"Where did you tell Ty he could find Nicole and Jim?" Hank asked in a whisper.

"They liked to meet at the pond on her daddy's farm. I used to follow him out there without them knowing I was in them woods. It was always in the same spot, so I knew exactly how to tell Ty to sneak up on them like I used to do."

"Did Ty kill Nicole?" Hank asked.

Rhonda shook her head fiercely. "She was a whore. It served her right."

"Did you see who killed her?" Hank asked.

"Tell us who did it," Agatha said.

"Ty."

CHAPTER THIRTEEN

THE TACO and Waffle was mostly empty at four o'clock, and it was about as private as they were going to get for this particular meeting. Agatha wasn't a hundred percent convinced Coil was completely on the up and up, but Hank trusted him, and Hank told her to trust his instincts because they'd never been wrong.

"Thanks for meeting us like this," Hank said to Coil as they waited for their table.

The hostess led the three of the to a table at the back of the restaurant.

"It's a slow day," Coil said, grinning. "Besides, I've known you a long time. I figured it was only a matter of time before you had something to tell me about that case."

Hank and Coil took the two seats that faced the front of the restaurant and Agatha sat across from them. She held the report from her computer in her hand.

"So what did you and Nancy Drew come up with?" Coil asked. "You're thinking I'm going to get burned with whatever you found in that report?"

"I sure hope not. But you're the sheriff and we trust you with the information."

"You know what my position is going to be on this, Hank. This is my agency, and no matter what it involves, I'm the one responsible. I'll always do what is right."

"I know. That's why we're friends." Hank took the file from Agatha and put it on the table. "When I started looking over the case files yesterday I noticed someone had cut off the page numbers of one of the reports and photo-copied it a second time to cover it up before giving it to Agatha. Someone didn't want Agatha to see whatever was in those reports. I got a chance to read the full report again, and I'll tell you that Lieutenant Earls did an outstanding job. Except I think he got too fixated on Walter Green as a suspect."

Coil blinked. "I'll agree with you on that. Personally, I think Earls wanted it to be Walter. There wasn't much good blood between them two."

"Here's where I'm going to apologize for duping you last night to get another copy of the report. We needed to not only see if the page numbers were missing, but what if anything inside the original report was changed from the one given us. Someone took great pains to substitute one page from the original. Because of that, they had to recreate a large portion of the rest of the report that followed the alteration." Hank said.

"Show me," Coil said, putting his hand on the file and pulling it toward him.

Hank let it go. It was the property of the sheriff's office after all.

"I hated to close that case without solving it," Coil said. "But there wasn't a choice. There were no more leads and no more resources. So I stuck it in a drawer and didn't touch it again until you asked for it, Agatha."

Hank watched as Coil opened the file, and he waited for his reaction. Agatha had marked the sections he needed to look at with a yellow highlighter.

"This doesn't make sense. What am I missing?"

"Look at the names," Hank said.

"All I can see is that the name Ty Lee is missing from the copy Agatha was given. He's listed as an associate of Nicole's, but not as a suspect. So what's the significance, and why go through the trouble of recreating an entire page?"

"Aggie?" Hank deferred to her.

"Ty Lee's mother, Kim Lee works for you," she said. "Right after Nicole's death, Ty applied to have his name legally changed to match his father's surname of Gunn. And now, Tyler Gunn works for you also."

Coil's mouth dropped open. "What? But why?"

"Easy," Agatha said. "Tyler was in love with Nicole, but she was sleeping with the same youth pastor that had knocked up Rhonda Mitchell. You convicted him of Rhonda's molestation, but you didn't know about Nicole. Of course, Rhonda knew about their affair, and was all too happy to tell Tyler where to find Nicole and the pastor in the woods. She set them up.

"So Tyler showed up at the pond just in time to witness their afternoon devotional, and Rhonda admits she was hiding in the woods watching the whole thing. Tyler went into a jealous rage, but he waited until the pastor left. And then he killed Nicole. He bashed her right in the head with the butt of his rifle."

Coil went pale and then color flooded into his cheeks. Hank knew he was furious. "This is unbelievable."

"Y'all did everything you could with what you had to work with. Lieutenant Earls covered the facts as y'all knew, but no one suspected that you had a rat on the inside. In the police report, Tyler's mom gave him his alibi. That's why he was never considered a suspect. She covered for him all along."

"I'll take care of it," Coil said. "Tyler and my chain-smoking secretary are about to find out what the inside of a cell looks like. I'll get with the county prosecutors about bringing charges against both of them. Rhonda too for not telling us she'd been a witness."

"If you would, you might reconsider that one," Agatha said. "She's a mess, and she's been through enough. It might do better if you order her to have weekly psych evaluations and get whatever meds she needs. She needs help. And she's got all those kids."

"If I can make a suggestion," Hank said.

"Might as well. This is your case now," Coil said. "What do you suggest?"

"That Aggie and I take this file back to your office tomorrow morning and give it back to her. Kim is going to know the second she sees it. She'll break easy enough. Once we have her confession you'll have enough to get an arrest warrant for Tyler."

Coil didn't take long to think about it. "That'll work. Kim takes her days off on Sunday and Monday, so she's always in the office on Saturday."

"Are the cameras at the station working?" Agatha asked.

"Yep. We'll make sure we've got a good recording."

"That settles it then," Hank said. "We'll see you at nine in the morning.

"Karl will be on duty," Coil said. "He'll let you in. It'll be easier if I'm not there for Kim to cling too."

It was eight-thirty the next morning, and as agreed, Agatha picked up Hank to drive him to the Bell County Sheriff's Office. Impatiently, she honked the horn once more. She knew Hank was probably moving slow that morning after having been up until about two o'clock rereading reports and making sure everything was correct. She was a bit groggy herself, but feeling a whole lot better than she had the night before.

Hank wore a pressed pair of khaki slacks and a navy blue polo. She recognized that he was going for a semi-official but relatable look. She was happy he'd retired his retirement clothes.

"Good morning, Aggie," Hank said, getting into the car.

"Morning, partner. You okay? You look a little tense."

"I never relax until its done. Completely done. Let's keep our guard up. There's still an armed and trained deputy who's been accused of murder on the loose."

That stark reminder reset her focus. They weren't going to pick up a blue ribbon, they were going to fight for justice. She nodded and drove them into town.

The Bell County Sheriff's Office was at the very end of Main Street. The single-story building had four parking spots across the front. Two for deputies, one for a guest and one with the name Kim Lee. Her silver Buick Oldsmobile sat parked there as it always did.

"This is going to be hard. She was friends with my mom," Agatha said.

"I'm sorry," was all he could say.

They walked in, and Karl was waiting as assigned. He was serious and looked more mature in his pressed deputy's uniform. The six-point star was pinned proudly on his chest

His duty was to remain close by in the event that Tyler stopped in. Other than that, he wasn't to sit directly in on the meeting. Someone had to keep up with phone calls to the switchboard while Agatha and Hank met with Kim in the small conference room.

"Hi there, Kim," Agatha said.

"Oh, hello Agatha. You back again so soon?" Kim's hands shook as she smashed out a cigarette butt in her overflow ashtray.

"Yes, ma'am. We came by to speak with you."

Kim peeked at Coil's door, but it was still locked.

"We'd like to see just you. Not Sheriff Coil." Hank interjected a sense of authority to make sure Kim's attempt at familiar sympathy wasn't successful on Agatha.

Kim fiddled with the phone. "I'm really busy today. Could you come back later? Maybe schedule an appointment."

"Karl will take your place while you're on break." Agatha said.

Kim looked at Karl nervously and then back at Hank and Agatha. She was in her late fifties, and she'd gone slightly plump with age. Her dark brown hair was teased around her head like a football helmet.

She and Hank followed Kim into the small room. It was maybe ten by ten, but the closeness worked to their advantage. Agatha blinked at Hank and he nodded for her to go forward.

"Now Kim," she said, "This isn't going to be easy for any of us, but we feel enough time has passed and the truth needs to come out. Justice needs to be served."

"I'm confused." She tapped her fingers on her leg nervously.

"I can help with that," she said. Agatha spread both reports on the table.

Kim's eyes blinked rapidly as tears formed in the corners of them. She was no hardened criminal that needed to be broken. She was a broken mother who'd tried to save her son.

Agatha waited for her to compose herself. But Kim didn't deny any of it. She didn't proclaim her innocence or try to run. She just looked...defeated.

"Why?" Agatha asked softly.

"He's my boy. My only child," Kim said, shrugging. "I never knew for sure if he killed her, but I suspected. There was blood on the butt of his rifle, and he was gone that day. I knew they'd take him away and lock him up. He was all I had left. So I told Tyler it'd be simpler all around if he let me handle it and said we were both home together. So I handled it."

"Do you know why he killed her?" Hank asked.

"We never spoke of what happened," she said, staring blankly at them. "After they closed the case we just pretended like it never happened. Like he never knew her." She folded and unfolded an old napkin. "He's my son. My only child?"

"Yes, ma'am," Agatha said softly. "We know."

"What's going to happen to my baby?" There was still a hopeful look in her eyes that was devastating to see.

"Sheriff Coil and the Texas Rangers are bringing him in," Hank said. "The best thing he can do is cooperate and do the right thing."

Kim nodded and the tears she was trying to hold back started to fall. "I did the best I could," she said, sobbing softly. "It was just the two of us and I did my best. But I guess my best wasn't good enough."

EPILOGUE

THERE WAS a restlessness in Hank's spirit, even more so than usual. Law enforcement was in his blood. But just because he retired didn't mean his thirst for it would go away. No, it had been time to let it go. It was a younger man's game. But there were other things he could do. Agatha had helped him realize that. His instincts and expertise were too valuable to let go to waste.

The morning breeze was beginning to fade and the heat was creeping in as the sun rose higher in the sky. He'd lost track of the time and was enjoying the solitude—enjoying letting his mind consider the possibilities.

The birds were playing in the birdbath he'd set up in the shade, and he propped his legs up on the ottoman, relaxing against the cushioned wicker chair. He analyzed his choice of pajama pants—the soft cotton plaid in red and gray—and he decided Agatha would deem them retirement-worthy.

Hank froze when he heard footsteps shuffling through the grass and the snap of a twig. He didn't move from his chair, but he grabbed his Glock and held it casually in his lap, waiting for whoever was at his gate to announce themselves.

"You back here, Hank?" Coil called out. "I tried the door, but nobody answered."

"I'm here," he said. "Come on back."

Coil opened the wooden gate and came into Hank's sanctuary. And then he saw the gun and grinned.

"Don't shoot. I'd hate to have to explain it to my wife."

Hank smiled in return and put the gun back on the bench where he'd taken it from.

"Help yourself to a drink," Hank said, pointing to the outdoor mini fridge. It was stocked with water and diet sodas. "Or I've got coffee in the house."

"I'm good with water," Coil said, grabbing one and taking the seat across from Hank.

"You're out early for a Sunday morning," Hank said. "I thought you took Sundays off?"

Coil took a long drink and then stretched out his legs, crossing his snakeskin boots. His plaid shirt was pressed and his jeans were new. He was freshly shaved and his hair was still damp at the collar.

"I had a couple of things to wrap up at the office. Yesterday wasn't exactly a normal day," he said, tipping his water toward Hank. "So I figured I'd get up and then swing back by the house to pick up Shelly and the kids for church."

"Hank, are you back here?" Agatha called out from the other side of the fence.

He grinned at the sound of her voice. Suddenly his private sanctuary wasn't so private anymore. But it didn't bother him like it normally would.

"Yep, come on back," he called out, but she was already opening the gate.

She was wearing a pair of hot pink nylon jogging shorts with lime green trim and a lime green racerback tank that proclaimed her love of cake. Hank had never noticed how long her legs were before. He looked away quickly and took a drink of his own water.

"I was finishing up my run and saw Coil's truck out front. Everything okay?"

"Everything is good. I just had to finish up some stuff at the office and thought I'd stop by and get a first-hand glimpse of what retired life is like." Coil looked around and grinned. "I've got to say, it doesn't seem too bad. Though those pajama pants have to go."

Agatha snickered and grabbed a water from the fridge, taking a seat in one of the other cushioned wicker chairs.

"I've got to tell you," she said. "I'm having a hard time wrapping my head around this whole thing. I didn't sleep at all last night."

"I think we're all a bit shell shocked," Coil said. "It's not every day you have to arrest a cop you've mentored and trained. And I can say for sure it's something I never want to do again."

"It'll take a while for the community to recover too," Hank said. "Kim and Tyler were loved by a lot of people around here."

"You know," Coil said. "I've been thinking maybe you two have something special. Nicole Green's murder isn't the only cold case around here.

Hank got caught in Agatha's gaze. Had her eyes always been that pretty shade of bluish green? "What do you think, Aggie?"

"I think you call me Aggie to annoy me. And I think I have to finish this book before I do much else." She paused and took another sip of water. "But I'm open to the suggestion."

"What about you, Coil?" Agatha asked. "How are you doing through all this?"

Coil shook his head and it was impossible to miss the myriad of emotions that crossed his face—sadness and anger being the most prominent.

"I think this was my fault. I was so fixed on it being her daddy that the real murderer not only got away with it, but he came to work right under my nose. How arrogant is that? Maybe what happened in Austin messed me up more than I thought. Or maybe I'm not the cop I thought I was."

Hank understood how Coil was feeling. When you were in charge, the responsibility lied with you. It was a heavy burden to bear.

"You did your job," Hank said. "Sometimes the facts we're given is all we have to work with. It throws a wrench in the works when the people we trust lie and alter the facts. You can't know everyone's deepest secrets or their pain. Look how many people suffered loss because of this.

We can only take the facts known to us and do the best we can to piece them together until the puzzle is complete. You didn't have all the pieces of the puzzle. And thank goodness you didn't try to force the pieces to point to Walter Green.

It would've been easy to do that and an innocent man would be in prison. Despite what your heart wanted, you did the right thing."

"I failed to serve justice."

"No, my friend," Hank said. "Justice was slow, but it was indeed served."

SNEAK PEEK: A TISKET A CASKET

Download Now - A Tisket a Casket

October 29, 2010

Orange flames danced through the attic with viciousness—
devouring without prejudice—the monster growing in
power as it was fed. Plumes of black smoke swirled into the
night sky, and the flames hissed as powerful streams of
water tried to destroy the destroyer.

Red lights flashed through the streets, a disorienting
symphony of sounds and color. Everyone watched as the
battle raged on, wondering who would come out the victor.

The Rio Chino Fire Department was proud of its
history—a hundred and forty-five years of serving the public
and battling the monsters that threatened their community.

The house was old, nothing more than kindling for the
flames that ate it alive. They'd been called soon enough to
save some of the structure, but it was the fire department's
own demons that threatened to end the tradition of brother-
hood under fire.

Fire Chief Kip Grogan was a thirty-year vet with less than a year until a full and well-earned retirement. His silver shock of thinning hair and round, red cheeks made Kip easily identifiable on any fire scene. Tonight though, he was fighting more than fire.

"Lester, get some spray on the southwest corner. It's trying to hop houses." Kip ordered over the radio.

"Trying to sir, but Gage isn't cooperating."

"Gauge, what gauge? Everything's at full pump and pressure. Pour water where I told you."

"No, it's Gage, Gage McCoy. This is his house, and he's not letting us suppress it."

"Why not?" Kip yelled over the radio and sirens that wailed along the small suburban street.

"Said he lost it in his divorce and hopes it burns to the ground," Lester said.

"I don't care what he says," Kip said. "Arrest him."

"Except that I'm not a cop," Lester said. "He is. And he's armed."

The roar of the hoses fighting the fire was deafening, but Kip felt the chill cross over his skin—that internal warning that told him something was about to go very, very wrong. The sound of rushing water came to a halt and there was nothing but the sound of crackling flames.

"What's going on?" he yelled again. He kicked open the doors of the command center truck where he'd been giving orders and was greeted with the sight of 1754 Constantine Drive fully engulfed in flames. His men stood watching. Helpless.

It didn't take long for Kip to assess the situation and understand why everything had come to a halt. A man stood, silhouetted by flame and shadow, a rifle in his hands.

He and Gage McCoy had gone through trainings

together. They'd been friends. But he also knew the job changed a man. Divorce changed a man too, and Gage had gone through a doozy. But friend or no, Gage was putting lives at stake, and he was turning his back on the oath he'd promised to uphold. Well, Gage wasn't going to destroy the reputation of what he'd help build over the last thirty years.

"Tony."

"Yes, Kip?"

"Get my gun." Kip ordered.

"But the cops are on their way." Tony Leatherman, the battalion chief's second in command pleaded with Kip.

"Give it to me or get out of my command center." Kip challenged him.

Reluctant, Tony unlocked the diamond-plated metal cabin that also served as a bench seat. He unboxed Kip's 45 caliber pistol and handed it to his chief.

"I'll show that bastard to interfere in a fire fighting operation." Kip howled.

Kip hefted his bulk one step toward the back of the truck, and fell dead from the doorway and into a puddle of backwashed water.

Continue the Adventure with A Tisket a Casket

Liliana and I have loved sharing these stories in our Harley & Davidson Mystery Series with you.

There are many more adventures to be had for Aggie and Hank. Make sure you stay up to date with life in Rusty Gun, Texas by signing up for our emails.

Thanks again and please be sure to leave a review where you bought each story and, recommend the series to your friends.

Kindly,
Scott & Liliana

Enjoy this book? You can make a big difference

Reviews are so important in helping us get the word out about Harley and Davidson Mystery Series. If you've enjoyed this adventure Liliana & I would be so grateful if you would take a few minutes to leave a review (it can be as short as you like) on the book's buy page.

Thanks,
Scott & Liliana

ALSO BY LILIANA HART

The MacKenzies of Montana

Dane's Return

Thomas's Vow

Riley's Sanctuary

Cooper's Promise

Grant's Christmas Wish

The MacKenzies Boxset

MacKenzie Security Series

Seduction and Sapphires

Shadows and Silk

Secrets and Satin

Sins and Scarlet Lace

Sizzle

Crave

Trouble Maker

Scorch

MacKenzie Security Omnibus 1

MacKenzie Security Omnibus 2

JJ Graves Mystery Series

Dirty Little Secrets

A Dirty Shame

Dirty Rotten Scoundrel

Down and Dirty

Dirty Deeds

Dirty Laundry

Dirty Money

A Dirty Job

Addison Holmes Mystery Series

Whiskey Rebellion

Whiskey Sour

Whiskey For Breakfast

Whiskey, You're The Devil

Whiskey on the Rocks

Whiskey Tango Foxtrot

Whiskey and Gunpowder

Books by Liliana Hart and Scott Silverii

The Harley and Davidson Mystery Series

The Farmer's Slaughter

A Tisket a Casket

I Saw Mommy Killing Santa Claus

Get Your Murder Running

Deceased and Desist

Malice In Wonderland

Tequila Mockingbird

Gone With the Sin

The Gravediggers

The Darkest Corner

Gone to Dust

Say No More

Lawmen of Surrender (MacKenzies-1001 Dark Nights)

1001 Dark Nights: Captured in Surrender

1001 Dark Nights: The Promise of Surrender

Sweet Surrender

Dawn of Surrender

The MacKenzie World (read in any order)

Trouble Maker

Bullet Proof

Deep Trouble

Delta Rescue

Desire and Ice

Rush

Spies and Stilettos

Wicked Hot

Hot Witness

Avenged

Never Surrender

Stand Alone Titles

Breath of Fire

Kill Shot

Catch Me If You Can

All About Eve

Paradise Disguised

ALSO BY LOUIS SCOTT

The Shepherd (#2)

Geaux Tiger (#3)

Cajun Cooking (#4)

Crooked Cross (#5)

Cracked Cross (#6)

Double Cross (#7)

Creole Crossroads (#8)

Bayou Backslide: Special Novella Edition

Bayou Roux: The Complete First Season

F.O.R.C.E Adventure Series

The Darkest Hour

Split Second

New York Minute

Liliana Hart is a New York Times, USAToday, and Publisher's Weekly bestselling author of more than sixty titles. After starting her first novel her freshman year of college, she immediately became addicted to writing and knew she'd found what she was meant to do with her life. She has no idea why she majored in music.

Since publishing in June 2011, Liliana has sold more than six-million books. All three of her series have made multiple appearances on the New York Times list.

Liliana can almost always be found at her computer writing, hauling five kids to various activities, or spending time with her husband. She calls Texas home.

If you enjoyed reading *this*, I would appreciate it if you would help others enjoy this book, too.

Lend it. This e-book is lending-enabled, so please, share it with a friend.

Recommend it. Please help other readers find this book by recommending it to friends, readers' groups and discussion boards.

Review it. Please tell other readers why you liked this book by reviewing. If you do write a review, please send me an email at lilianahartauthor@gmail.com, or visit me at http://www.lilianahart.com.

Connect with me online:
www.lilianahart.com
lilianahartauthor@gmail.com

facebook.com/LilianaHart

twitter.com/Liliana_Hart

instagram.com/LilianaHart

bookbub.com/authors/liliana-hart

Liliana's writing partner and husband, Scott blends over 25 years of heart-stopping policing Special Operations experience.

From deep in the heart of south Louisiana's Cajun Country, his action-packed writing style is seasoned by the Mardi Gras, hurricanes and crawfish étouffée.

Don't let the easy Creole smile fool you. The author served most of a highly decorated career in SOG buying dope, banging down doors, and busting bad guys.

Bringing characters to life based on those amazing experiences, Scott writes it like he lived it.

Lock and Load – Let's Roll.